THE BARD

THE BARD

Tales from Aévan: Book One

MATRELL WOOD

THE AHNDRIAN ARCHIVES

EVERY LIFE IS A STORY

The Ahndrian Archives

Contents

Dedicated to my family. Those by blood and those I chose. Even when I thought I could not, you all never let me forget that I could.

I

Prologue

Those summer mornings that wake you in pools of your own sweat were never something I found myself accustomed to. The blinding rays of sunlight that filter through the unnecessary windows placed upon the walls of my small home do little except irritate my already unbalanced psyche. I hate the things that bring joy to these illiterate fools that howl back to the morning calls of the roosters perched upon their fencepost and barn houses, giving thanks to the ancestors that sit back and watch as we do nothing but slaughter each other and begin, again and again, war after senseless war.

I say all this to note my ordinary condition while assuring you that I am not as pessimistic as these thoughts might lead you to believe. Here in Aévan the land can transition from fields of golden grain bathed in the warmth of the hallowed sun, to dismal plains of war-torn battlefields that grow nothing more than misery in those that gaze upon the bloodstained filth and ruins many once called home.

It is not as though this life has given me nothing. I have

my life; I married once before to the most beautiful Ahndaele to ever grace a battlefield, then married in my later years, after the death of the first wife, to another incredibly beautiful and fierce Ahnda woman. I have a beautiful daughter, and though we lost contact for many years, she has come back to me and saved me in ways I was unaware existed. I have had my life endangered and threatened on more than one occasion and found the strength in those around me to fight back and crush my enemies underfoot without so much as a shred of remorse, and all so those who look upon me could call me a *hero* and a *savior*. I hate these words, I hate their sentiments, and hate that I am none of these things they speak of.

I have my education, which allows me to read, write, and speak the language of my people, the Ahnda, and of your people, or at least one or two of your many common tongues. A language with which I am able to recount my story to you and hope you understand it and learn from my mistakes, though some words will never be spoken in your languages. For instance, the name of my people, the Ahnda, which could only be loosely translated as *the people of power*. That encompasses nothing of importance to who we are, for people of power exist within your world as well. There are those who exist off symbolic power, your kings, and queens much like our own rulers, but there are those who share Ahnda blood and have become known as the Ahndri. They are mere shadows to those who exist in Aévan, our home world. Something so far apart from your own that you may never truly understand it, but it exists, and it is so horrendously beautiful and ugly, and welcoming, and decrepit.

My story, my life in Aévan, is the only way I can help you,

no, make you understand that I am no pessimist, but merely realistic about the state of our world. I will tell you of the loss of my first wife, Alandriel, a woman who should have, at the very least, seen her death on the battlefields in which she earned her title as the Mistress of Mercy, or rather in sickness, upon her deathbed in the century she could have lived further. I will tell you of my search for my beloved daughter over the vast lands that span between Astoria, Illyori, Thelden, and Reissgard. These cities, our four capitals where any person may find themselves part of a long and bloody war. You will also come to know how all of this led to the discovery of my new love, my new wife, and the reasons that she is the only thing that kept me alive to this point.

I would be remised if I did not say it once more and disheartened if you did not heed these words. I am no pessimist. I do see the beauty this world offers. I see the joy in the laugh of the children that prance through the city streets and the love of those families which prosper despite the hard times. I am no pessimist, but there is nothing I see more than the blood that has been spilled in this beautiful disaster we call home.

2

The Drunken Brawler

"Yeah, I saw him there. Prancing about under the light of the storehouse like he owned the place." Magnus tossed back the rest of his ale and looked out at the curious onlookers who wanted nothing more than the rest of his tale. "When they called me and told me the weapons storehouse was being robbed, I figured that it had to be someone of some rapport at least. Imagine my surprise when it was that sluggish brute, Narcieum."

A chorus of laughter rang out from the other guardsmen and women gathered in the common area. They raised their glasses in praise of the return of their favorite storyteller. The room was filled with joy and celebration, but Magnus still couldn't bring himself to join in on the merriment. Nevertheless, he entertained them, if only to keep their worries at bay.

"Tell us about the takedown!" one half-drunken soldier called out from the back of the room.

His statement was met with a roar of approval and badgering from the rest of the crowd. Magnus lifted his hands above his head to quiet the room and leaned in closer.

"I tracked that big oaf from the storehouse all the way back to his petty little gang's hideout right outside the city walls. I mean, this place is a shithole," he gestured to the room, "but I swear this could be the damn palace compared to their hovel."

Another chorus of laughter. Magnus knew his joke wasn't that funny, but none of them could resist when he was telling his stories.

"I walked right in after him without a second thought. Just me and my fist. They boasted and cracked wise at my arrival, but their grandstanding was so short-lived I could barely remember a word they said. Three on my right came at me with daggers brandished. What a joke they were. By the time the rest of them came at me, I swear I had time for damn smoke."

"Urrr a madmen, Ma'nus." Another drunken guardsman slurred.

"The only one among us walkin' round without a lick of armor." Another added.

"'Cept that pretty captain he trained. That's an Ahndaele I'd like to-," said the half-drunk soldier from before.

"I wouldn't finish that statement, Boram. Lest I have to cut that tongue from your maw." Neoma scowled at him with her hand on the hilt of her sword.

All the others in the room cackled at the terror painted on Boram's face. Even Magnus joined in as he hopped from his seat atop the bar and embraced Neoma.

"Ah, come to join in the merriment, my dear?" Magnus asked.

Neoma could smell the stench of blood, alcohol, and sweat-drenched in his tunic. She stepped back and wrenched her nose away, uncertain if he was just met in battle or the brothel.

"I see you're in a state again. Come with me. I need to speak with you privately," Neoma said.

"Fine, fine. It's about time for me to head home anyway." Magnus turned to his crowd of admirers and bowed ungracefully. "Until dusk settles again, ponder over the wicked deeds I inflicted upon Narcieum."

Everyone cheered his boisterous exit and Magnus left the room with a false face painted with an amused smile. Neoma pushed through the throng of drunk men and women prattling on by the exit and stepped out into the darkened streets of Astoria. The roads were all but abandoned outside of the guardsmen quarters. A few stragglers slumped home from a late night, but most others were already in their homes or safely snuggled in bed. A few on-duty guards saluted the two squad captains as they made their way back to Magnus's villa.

Magnus watched Neoma's back as she walked ahead of him. Of course, she had no doubts as to their path. She'd spent so many years dragging him from that dusty old common room that he was positive she likely knew the way to his home better than he did. He felt guilty for the state she often found him in, but his sensibilities often felt out of his control. If not for her unique aversion to armor, much like his own, she likely would have abandoned him the moment she found out the truth of her former mentor. Though he was a handful of years beyond her, she far surpassed him in maturity, and he was fully aware of that fact.

They trekked the winding streets for another few minutes before walking up the steps of his home. Magnus slumped past Neoma and dropped into the comfort of his armchair without care. Neoma stormed into the courtyard and unsheathed her shortsword. She swung it at the practice stands scattered about the courtyard. Magnus raised an eyebrow and pushed himself from his chair.

"I thought you wanted to speak to me, not duel inanimate objects in the night." Magnus stepped over the threshold of the den into the courtyard.

"I do." She grunted between swings. "However, I am releasing my anger at your irreputable behavior before I say something I may come to regret."

Magnus stumbled into the center of the courtyard and stood behind her as she continued to slash into the training stands.

"What about my behavior makes you so angry, hmm? Is this not how I normally behave? I'd have thought you of all people would have been used to this by now."

Neoma screamed and turned to swing her blade at Magnus. He ducked her blade and caught her arm on the backswing, shoving her backward with one swift motion. She came at him again with rage coloring her eyes. Despite his state, Magnus ducked, blocked, and countered every swing of her sword.

"Do you perhaps need to jam your blade through my innards before you can speak your mind?"

"Shut up! I'm so sick of this childish behavior, Magnus." Neoma jammed her sword into the ground and glared at her former mentor. "It has been sixteen years. I do not deny that your sorrow is well reasoned, but you cannot continue to act this way."

Magnus returned her glare in earnest. His voice raised in volume and lowered in pitch as he stomped forward to meet her.

"Do not tell me how I should act!" His chest rose and fell rapidly. "My wife was murdered, and my daughter stolen from me. How, pray tell, do you expect me to simply move past this?"

"Your daughter could still be out there. If she were to be found. If she were to return home, how do you think she would react to see her father in such a state?" Neoma retorted.

Magnus fumed off across the courtyard and into the kitchen. He pulled a bottle of liquor from the cupboard and a glass from the shelf. He slammed them down in front of himself and stared at them both shakily. His vision blurred as tears began to form in his eyes. Neoma walked over and placed her hand on his. The anger on her face had turned to worry.

"Every time I close my eyes, I see his face," Magnus whispered. "I see him snatching my little girl from that damned cabin. I see Alandriel... I see-."

"They told me how she was found. It was horrible, I know, but Magnus this is destroying you. It has been for all this time and the more you let it, the more powerful Cade becomes in your mind."

"Horrible doesn't begin to describe what I saw beside that lake. He strung her up like a scarecrow and hung her out for all to see. Horror is far more kind than what I witnessed that day." Magnus dropped his hands from the glass and bottle.

He slumped across the kitchen and settled into a chair at the end of the dining table. Neoma nestled into the closest chair and they sat in silence until Magnus was ready to speak again.

"In truth, I don't know why it still eats at me so heavily after all this time. I don't think this pain is misbegotten, but I have tried so dearly to seek forgiveness from the elders and all of my prayers seem to fall upon deaf ears."

"Why would you think you need forgiveness? It was not you who slew the Mistress of Mercy. She was your wife. You loved her. Cade is the one who took her life. Do not hate yourself. Hate him." Neoma placed her hand on his once more, but when she looked into his eyes, she knew he was not looking back at her.

"It is all my fault. That much I know. It was I who suggested we take to Crowind. I wanted so much to get away from this damnable city. I brought us there and it led the Emerald Blood right to us. I knew they hated her, but I didn't think they'd come for us there. I was naive."

Neoma sighed and dropped her gaze. She fully realized why he drowned so heavily in his sorrows. Had both Alandriel and his daughter been slain, he likely would have continued hurting, but he would have resolved to some semblance of his former life. However, with his daughter's kidnapping, a pang of lingering guilt that she could have been, or may well still be, subjected to many horrors by the hands of Cade and the Emerald Blood. He wasn't simply accosting himself for what was, he was plagued by thoughts of what could be.

3

Invitation from a Shadow

Magnus found himself waking in his bed without a single thought as to how he got there. Now sober, he could smell the filth of the night before lingering on his clothes. He stripped himself bare and walked to the bathhouse. The sunlight streaming in from the skylights assaulted his already aching senses. The water cascaded from the faucet and the noise filled the quiet around him with a soothing rhythm. He lowered himself into the bath and laid his head back as he waited for the water level to rise.

His mind trailed off to the past as it had done every day for the last sixteen years. He remembered the days before their trip; the wonderful smiles of his wife, Alandriel, and his newborn daughter. Before they came into his life, he never sought anything but the rush of the battle and the joy of telling stories. Then they became his entire life, and so shortly after they were taken from him.

Perhaps Neoma was right, he thought to himself as the water rose to his chest.

The first four years after losing his family, he searched everywhere he could reach to find his daughter, but Cade and the bandit guild known as the Emerald Blood had simply vanished without a trace. Not one word came from any of his scouts or the many war parties sent out by the kingdom to avenge their Mistress of Mercy. With no trace of Cade, the trail to find his daughter had run cold, and Magnus was left with nothing but his sorrows. So, he drowned them.

The last decade was spent in an alcohol-induced stupor at every chance he could achieve such a state. Only six years ago did the commander of the Astorian Royal Guard put together his plan to force Magnus back on his feet. Six years ago, Neoma joined the guard after winning the Sword Festival tournament. She had a similar aversion to the heavy armors the rest of the Royal Guard wore and so she was placed into Magnus's care. She was like Alandriel in so many ways. Her fervor in battle was unmatched; her tenacity when the odds were stacked against her; her skill with a blade and prowess in combat. She was the ultimate warrior in every sense of the word.

However, it was not just the warrior that Magnus admired. Despite her tendency to use violence to solve many situations, she was also quite gentle when her words could solve more than her sword. She was far more intelligent than he, and when he seemed to be at his lowest, she never hesitated to stand by his side. She had become a dear friend. Perhaps more, but Magnus couldn't bring himself to accept anything else. He stared at his hands and saw only blood. As the cage he'd built inside his own mind closed in around him, he refused to trap someone else in the prison of his own making.

Magnus reached forward and turned the faucet shut when the water reached up to his shoulders. He let out a deep sigh and sank back into its warmth. His home was quiet once more. Just far enough outside the residential district that the early morning hustle lent no chorus to the music of nature surrounding him. He grabbed the soap and went to work cleansing yesterday from his skin. Sorrow filled his heart once more as memories of Alandriel rushed forward and he imagined her hands caressing his skin as she always did. He imagined looking into her deep brown eyes. He remembered the glow of her tawny-brown skin, how wonderful it felt against his fingertips. He pictured her bright smile igniting his heart every morning when he opened his eyes.

Tears began to mix with the water of the bath and before long he pushed himself out of the bath, wrapped himself in a towel, and walked over to the kitchen cabinet. He stared at the counter where he left the bottle and glass from the night before. His hands hung limp at his sides and despite the furious urge to drown this pain, Neoma's words cut deep into his mind. Perhaps she had such an effect on him because they were so similar, yet so different that she pulled him into an entirely different space. If not for knowing their family histories, he imagined they could have been sisters, born of different fathers or mothers.

Magnus trudged over to the nearest chair and dropped without care.

"Alandriel," His words floated through the empty room, "I simply do not know what to do. You asked me to protect her before you stood your ground and I failed you. What has become of our little girl?"

He waited in silence for what felt like an eternity before resigning himself to seek out the rest of his day. He marched back to his room and donned a fresh set of pants and a clean tunic. He wrapped his hands in his usual cloth and donned a dark cloak before stepping over the threshold into the glaring sun outside.

Magnus hesitated as he took the first steps from his door. He had not seen the world through sober eyes in many months. Everything seemed louder. Everything was far too bright and moved with reckless abandon. He wondered if he truly preferred reality with dulled senses. He caught a glimpse of the cook for the nearby inn and set his mind on getting his stomach filled before making any other decisions about the coming hours.

"Marshall!" Magnus called from across the road.

"Aye, Master Magnus. You seem in better spirits this morning."

"Simply hunting for my morning's fill. Heading in to fire up the range?"

Marshall nodded and gestured for Magnus to follow him up the road. Magnus watched as Marshall walked with purpose, smiling, and waving at every person that passed within ten feet of him. Compared to him, Magnus was little more than dull moonlight to the radiance in Marshall's smile. He couldn't help but see the truth in such a thought. Not one person that passed by seemed happy to lay eyes on Magnus. Most days he might not have paid it any mind, but Neoma's words continued to weigh on his mind.

"That cursed woman," Magnus grunted under his breath.

They pushed through the doors of the Frost Foot Inn and the calmness of the interior relieved the strain on Magnus's senses.

"Take a seat at the bar. I'll whip you up something."

Marshall walked past the front and left Magnus to his own devices. He sat on the nearest barstool and looked over the bar's interior to pass the time. The owner spent considerable time in the inn's upkeep, and it was not without recognition. The Frost Foot was one of the oldest lodgings in Astoria, but the state of the place would never give up its age. The walls stood without rot or damage and the plethora of pictures hanging about the place were absent of even a speck of dust. Every table and barstool looked newly crafted. The only piece of the inn that could be considered in disrepair was the bar itself. Wilheda, the inn's capricious owner wanted to keep the original bar as long as it would hold. There were names of famous Ahndaele carved into various areas of the bar and it was the Frost Foot's most important bit of history.

Magnus ran his hand over the carving of his own name beneath that of Alandriel's. A sad smile spread across his face and he chuckled at the thought of their drunken night carving their names with a fork after their meal.

"She was a fine Ahndaele. Though I'm still not sure why you carved your name into the bar," Wilheda said.

Magnus looked up to find her leaning on the bar in front of him. He pulled his hand from the bar and straightened himself up.

"I'm no Ahndaele, but I'm a warrior nonetheless."

"Well that's as true as it could be, I suppose." Wilheda

grabbed a clean glass from under the bar and set it in front of Magnus. "The usual?"

Magnus held a hand up and shook his head. "Not today. Made a promise for the day."

"You made a promise to take a day off the bottle? Who could get you to keep a promise like that?"

"Myself."

Wilheda looked Magnus over. She shrugged and set the glass back under the bar. "Marshall! Get that damned kitchen fired up before I fire your ass!"

Marshall burst through the kitchen door with a plate of eggs, sausage, and bread as though on cue. He set the plate in front of Magnus and gave him a quick nod and a wink. He turned to Wilheda and gave her a vicious smile.

"You keep threatening to fire me while I'm doing my job and I might have to take my services over to Stone Point."

Wilheda narrowed her eyes. "You wouldn't."

Marshall shrugged and let out a hearty laugh before disappearing to the back. Magnus chuckled and dug into his breakfast. Marshall's cooking never disappointed. About halfway through his meal the door of the inn creaked open and a tangible silence fell over the room. Magnus felt the shift in the atmosphere and peered over his shoulder. A man in a shadowy cloak walked through the doorway and headed straight for him. Magnus let out a deep sigh and went back to his breakfast.

The cloaked man sat at the bar next to him and pulled back his hood. His face was no more terrifying than the average man, but it was the eyes of deep crimson that always made others avert their gaze from the shadows.

"Elias, you know your kind aren't welcome in places where people generally find themselves happy."

"You think you're so clever, don't you? Believe me," Elias peered around the room at the throng of onlookers who stared at his back, "I'd rather not step foot in this hovel again, but I came to fetch you."

Magnus swallowed the last of his breakfast and turned to face Elias. "What business could you possibly have with me?"

"King Mirian has requested the presence of you and that Ahndaele Ves you trained. The three of us are to meet him in the king's court at midday. Don't be late."

Elias pushed out from the bar and walked out of the door without another word. Magnus set his fork on the plate and placed a few coins on the bar. He gazed around the room and could see the discomfort Elias's presence had left. He waved at Wilheda and proceeded out the doorway.

A meeting with the king, he thought to himself. Someone's losing their head today. Let's hope it's an enemy.

4

The King of Bandits

Miryllyn paced back and forth through the guild hall study. The air around her was full of electricity and every hair on her body seemed to stand on end. The soft voices trickling down from the upper levels served little more than to irritate her already skewed anger.

"Either cease your incessant yammering or remove yourselves at once!" She screamed to her guild members.

The sound of their chairs scraping against the newly refurbished wooden floors and the scampering footsteps heading to the exit drew a blissful sigh from her aching chest. She walked around to the side of a nearby table and placed herself precariously on its edge. The room was full of nothing. Nothing except the sound of her own breathing and it was all she could seem to handle as the day dragged on.

As the hours passed by, she found herself moving from the edge of the table to one of the cushioned chairs in the corner of the room. She tilted her head back and closed her eyes, letting the dark oak interior fade away to nothingness. She was oblivious to the world around her and wanted only a moment of peace before setting out again to find the ring that she had seemingly misplaced.

"Quite the unusual place to be resting, Miryllyn." Cade's deep, raspy voice shook her from the unplanned slumber she had fallen into.

"Oh m—Sir, I'm so sorry. I wanted to rest my legs for a moment. I had not realized how much time had passed." She jumped to her feet and threw her arm across her chest in a rigid salute.

A hearty laugh escaped Cade's throat, sending tremors throughout the study. He placed a large pale hand on Miryllyn's shoulder and twisted his lips into a crooked grin.

"You've earned some rest, Lieutenant. I know it's been difficult planning for my upcoming wedding. You've shouldered the responsibility well."

She couldn't look him in the eye as he spoke. He was unaware of her recent blunder and she wasn't sure he would forgive her if he found out. It was true, he had given her the sole responsibility of the preparations for his marriage to the witch. She was certain that this was far beyond the scope of her abilities as someone who was raised in the Wildlands and knew only violence, but he had asked this of her and one could only imagine what would be forfeit if she let him down.

She bowed her head. "Everything will be ready by the end of the month as you have requested sir. I have everything handled."

"Oh," Cade tilted his head, and his crooked grin grew malicious, "is that so? So, there have been no issues thus far?"

Miryllyn's eyes widened, but she kept them pointed to the

floor. She took a deep breath and relaxed her face, before meeting his gaze with stern assurance.

"Nothing at all, sir."

Cade's pleased expression turned sour and his hand shot forward and wrapped tightly around her throat. She clawed at his hands and gasped for air as he squeezed tighter.

"Funny," he stared into her horror filled eyes without a hint of concern, "because I just received word that a therostone ring, *my* therostone ring, was just recovered from a pickpocket in the Barrows. Seems a young boy felt his fingers were quite light when you were in the market earlier today. Though I suppose that thought no longer crosses his mind."

"I'm sorry, sir. I did not mean to deceive you." She choked out the words as she continued to cling to her fading consciousness.

"And yet, you attempted to do just that. It's a pity really. I had grown quite fond of you. I even considered making you my second in command after the wedding. Now it seems you are entirely unfit for such a position." He loosened his grip and let her fall to the floor.

She coughed and sputtered, drawing in sharp, painful breaths with tears in her eyes. She could feel the bruises forming beneath her skin and the blood settling in her throat.

"I will accept whatever punishment you give me, sir," her breath rasped in her throat.

Cade turned his back to her and walked towards the exit with his hands snug in his pockets. "Don't disappoint me again. I shall hold onto the ring for now. Continue with the rest of the preparations."

He slammed the door shut behind him without another

word. Miryllyn gripped the edge of the chair she had been sleeping in moments ago and lifted herself up from the floor. The quiet put her at ease once more, but now the air was free of electricity and was only filled with the haunting energy that filled her when she thought her life would come to an end in this darkened corner.

She had never felt such a deep terror in all her days. Despite years on the battlefield — from childhood, as a young woman, and well into her later years — and even when her mother told her stories of the Fade as a little girl, she never knew terror before she met Cade. His presence could likely bring the Night Riders to their knees when next they brought the Fade at their backs.

When he found her, he promised her glory in the ranks of the Emerald Blood, but now she wasn't sure that leaving the Wildlands was the choice she should have made after her village was razed, her family slaughtered by a neighboring tribe. She shook away her doubts and marched to the exit, fear and anger carrying her feet across the room. She would find her death in battle, amongst her brothers-in-arms amidst chaos where she thrived. It would not be alone in some sad, dark little corner where no one would taste the sting of her blade. Even if her life depended on something as menial as a wedding, she would see it done before she allowed herself to fail. With that in mind, she was assured and prepared to finish what was asked of her.

Never again, she thought to herself as she pushed through the heavy oak door. *I'd rather take you with me.*

5

The Light of Hope

The marble steps leading up to the king's white stone castle loomed over Magnus with a menacing presence. He had not stepped foot in the king's court since he returned from Crowind all those years ago. Even then, he did not want to speak to anyone about the events he bore witness to. Now he was beckoned to return to those same wretched halls, where every person, from nobleman to courtesan, would bring their pitiful gaze to rest on him.

Step by step he ascended to the territory of the most powerful. His footsteps came to an abrupt halt when he reached the apex. The towering setirwood doors, dark as obsidian and tough as iron, remained open as though they beckoned him forward into the enticing grasp of the rich and influential. Magnus drew in a sharp breath and placed one foot in front of the other until he was over the threshold.

The halls were much like he remembered, though the effects of time showed lightly on the stone that encircled him. He noted the cracks as he moved. His mind focused solely on that purpose the further he pressed on. The distance to the smaller, but more ornate setirwood doors that stood between him and the court closed with each passing second. His heartbeat seemed to echo against the stone walls louder than his footsteps could manage. He was certain every servant and guard he passed could hear the pounding in his chest. Their eyes following his pace with pitied annoyance.

The two guards posted outside of the court lurched forward in a half-hearted bow. Magnus grunted in response to their forced civility. They straightened themselves and pulled on the roped handles of the door without a word to Magnus's unenthusiastic response. The doors crept open and gave way to the same beckoning he felt earlier. Inside he could see that everyone else had already gathered — Elias, Neoma, Erelwyn, and Prince Alluran Nightingale — poised in front of the throne where King Mirian Nightingale sat above all others with poise and power.

"Well, I must say I'm quite surprised you accepted my summons without more of a fuss, Magnus," King Mirian spoke.

Magnus held the same expressionless visage he wore the entire journey to the king's court, but with a heavy head, he stopped midway through the room and bowed as a subject was expected.

King Mirian laughed as he rose from his throne and descended his pedestal to meet Magnus. "Come now, Magnus. As Alluran's former swordmaster and, most importantly, my childhood friend, such proclivities are unnecessary in private gatherings such as this."

"I was unaware that this would be considered private,"

Magnus glanced around the room at the various eyes locked on him and the king, "given the positions of those present here. Your closest advisor, your son, and a shadow are all here. Hardly seems a casual affair."

The king's gaze dropped, and Magnus could see the twinge of sadness painting his features. No other in the room made a sound. Prince Alluran, usually a ball of energy having only seen sixteen cycles in his young life, looked solemn in Magnus's presence. However, the king's advisor, Erelwyn, remained as stoic as ever. Though Magnus could feel the enmity streaming off him like tendrils of smoke.

Magnus's abilities not only lent him the opportunity to induce emotion, but he could sense strong ones as well when there was no intention to conceal them. People were often wary around him for that fact. Things better left unknown were rarely hidden in his presence. However, it helped him be the leader that he was for his guardsmen. Now, that ability filled him with angst. Aside from the disapproval of Erelwyn, everyone else reeked of pity and worry.

"Perhaps there is something I should know, my King?" Magnus prodded, growing impatient.

King Mirian looked up at Erelwyn, who nodded reluctantly. "Yes, things are quite troubling, my friend. We received word little more than two nights ago, and we have just confirmed the legitimacy of this missive."

Erelwyn walked forward and handed Magnus a small scroll. Magnus looked up at the king, and upon receiving an approving nod, unraveled the message. His eyes grew wide and his teeth bared as the message came to a close. His entire body was shaking, but he dared not lose control in such a hallowed place. King Mirian sighed and placed a hand on Magnus's shoulder. Magnus fought the sudden urge to smack his hand away and race from the room with bloodlust driving his footsteps.

"My King, I don't think it needs to be said, but—"

"I would not dare advise you otherwise. However, I asked you here because I wanted to make a few things clear before you run off after the Emerald Blood." King Mirian gestured to his nearby council meeting table and asked everyone to sit.

When they were all placed in chairs, he continued. "This is the first time in sixteen long years that we have received any word of their movements. Their position near Grithala is indeed troubling. There are greater distances they could have placed between us and them. In truth it makes me wonder if this is a ploy to draw us out. However, we don't know what Cade has been up to these many years, and after the great disrespect he has shown this nation, I would be remiss if I did not have his bandits properly investigated."

"I understand your worries, King Mirian, but what is it that you ask of us?" Neoma said. "We are simply three. It is unlikely that they are traveling in an encampment of less than twenty."

"This is true. I have prepared orders for both of your units to deploy from the city. Elias will be traveling along with you. There is a scout stationed in the city that will meet you on the southern overlook of Grithala. He will give you whatever information he learns through his continued observation. Your orders are to capture at least one member of these criminals and wipe out the rest. If Cade is among them," his eyes fell on Magnus with stern conviction, "do with him what you wish."

Magnus narrowed his eyes and met the king's gaze. Something was very wrong with the emotions he could sense from the man he once called a friend. He could sense the animosity he felt towards Cade, but it wasn't that of a king feeling anger for his people. Something about it was more sinister, more personal. Magnus shunned the worries regardless of how out of place they seemed. This was the first opportunity he'd had in sixteen years to find Cade — to find his daughter — and he would not let it pass him by.

* * *

The sun crept beneath the horizon and brought an end to the tense afternoon that Magnus and Neoma spent informing their squads of their new orders. They sought the easiest solution by bringing them both together in the common area of the barracks and giving them all the information at once. Most of the Royal Guard was aware of Magnus's hatred of the Emerald Blood and the death of his wife, but the loss of his daughter was a detail left out of the conversation, and even he was unaware just how many people knew the whole truth.

For a long time, the guardsmen seemed unsure of their destination and the reason they had been chosen. Nevertheless, they refused to disobey orders given to them by their squad leaders and King Mirian. They received their marching orders, and they all spent the night prepping for the journey that would begin with the rising sun.

Magnus and Neoma retired to his villa for the night. Shadows clung to Neoma's features as they passed through the city streets. Her mind was far away from the present and her eyes locked onto some distant terror. Her left eye's foretelling gave her a distinct advantage on the battlefield, but uncertainty often filled her with dread, as she could not tell the future of things she could not see. She had never left the walls surrounding Astoria, never abandoned the relative safety that their towering presence provided them. She was strong, but in truth, she was quite sheltered.

Magnus watched her as they rounded the final corner towards his home. He balled his fists, digging his nails into his calloused palms. *What comfort could someone like me provide to one feeling such terror for the purpose of my own crusade?* He couldn't promise her protection. He knew even the most foolish of Ahndaele knew such promises were little more than fanciful words in romantic tales.

They stepped over the threshold into his home. Magnus led Neoma to the kitchen and pulled a glass from the cabinet. He grabbed the closest bottle of liquor and ripped the cork from the top of the bottle.

"Magnus, this is not the time for you to get drunk," Neoma said as he finished pouring and capped the bottle.

He set the glass on the countertop in front of her and walked towards the courtyard without a word. Neoma looked between the glass and his back. She moved her hand to the glass and realized for the first time that it was shaking. She knew that she was nervous about leaving the city, but with all her sight, she refused to acknowledge just how terrified she was to go up against a tyrant like Cade. She grabbed the glass of murky brown liquor and tossed it back in a single mouthful. She let the warmth of the liquid cascading down her throat bring her some comfort. She took a deep breath and turned to join Magnus in the courtyard.

Magnus was already whacking away at the training dummies. Despite his time spent in a drunken stupor, he was still relatively graceful in form and execution. However, his speed was far less impressive than it once was. Where he once could make ten strikes, only five now landed. Neoma drew her sword and slashed at the training dummy nearest him. Unable to help himself, Magnus glanced over at her and the mentor in him grew frustrated at the undisciplined form she was executing.

"Reposition your back leg as I showed you. You are far beyond the level to make such amateur mistakes."

Neoma smirked and corrected her form with little effort. "He speaks. I was wondering how long this awkward silence would persist."

Magnus let out the heavy breath that sat in his chest. He let out a small chuckle and gestured to Neoma to face off him with him in the center of the courtyard. She sheathed her sword and grabbed a practice sword from a nearby basket. They faced each other on opposite sides of the courtyard and took up their stances.

Neoma paced around, waiting to see if he would make the first move. She always struggled to match his speed, even when she could see the first two or three moves with her left eye. In his current state, she was sure she could keep him at a distance that benefited her sword over his fist. Magnus was aware of his reduced speed. However, he was certain he was fast enough to counter any blow she could swing his way, even with her foresight. However, her foresight was the main reason he hesitated to strike first. His reflexes were far too diminished and his strikes far less precise.

"You know, in all this time that you have taught me, you never once told me who it was that trained you," Neoma said.

"I wasn't. The academy tried to teach me to fight with a longsword and heavy armor. It never suited me. So, I would climb the academy gates at night and watch the bare-knuckle bouts in the lower sectors of the city."

"Why does it not surprise me that you failed to adhere to the rules your entire life?"

Magnus shrugged and gave a half-cocked smile. Neoma lunged while his form was off, but gasped when she realized she had been baited. Magnus ducked her thrust and struck her wrist with his palm before twirling around her sweeping her back leg from under her. She crashed to the ground and sucked in a sharp breath after the wind was knocked out of her. The mistake frustrated her, but she couldn't help but laugh at Magnus's smug grin.

"Those rules you speak of," he reached a hand down for her, "they exist to keep the criminal in check or the unimaginative in line. If a rule causes no harm or trouble for another, it was made to be broken."

Neoma gripped his hand and pulled him to the ground. She dropped her leg across him and mounted him. She placed the point of the wooden sword on his chest and pressed it down with enough force to cause a small red ring to appear on his skin.

"Here I thought after all this time you had nothing left to teach me," Neoma said as her chest heaved with every breath she took.

"I fell for a classic. I'd almost be impressed, but you made one mistake." Magnus slid his leg between hers and flipped her over. "You forgot to secure my limbs and strengthen your position. If your opponent is not dead, then assume they're not done fighting. Every move you make must serve a purpose. Leave no holes in that purpose or they will be exploited."

Neoma gathered herself and faced off with him once more. "So, why bare-knuckle brawls? If you didn't want to use a sword, could you not have learned from an Ahndaele Tik instead? Before you, a close-range fighter without armor was unheard of in the guard. Even then, I was the only one to follow your example."

"I attempted that route first. However, my power was deemed unsuitable for an Ahndaele. They were unsure of even letting me into the academy with a power that would show me no benefit in battle. It was King Mirian, when he was only the prince, who convinced the headmaster to allow me to train under the Ahndaele Ves. I had none of the range of Tik abilities and no control like Fey. Steel was the only option they thought I could manage."

Neoma struck again. Her swings were simple this time as she found herself more curious as to how this story continued. "That still doesn't explain the lack of a weapon in your hands. Even a rapier or staff seems more intelligent at the end of the day."

Magnus ducked her swings with ease and countered her wide arcing slashes whenever she tried to catch him off balance. He ducked into her final swing, letting the sword graze his left shoulder before catching the hilt with the back of his hand. He followed with his right, slamming his palm against her arm, forcing her to drop her sword.

"I tried them all. However, it was in those bouts that I

saw what a true warrior looked like. Not only maneuvering around blows and blocking those they could not dodge. They took each hit in stride and came at their opponent with their whole self. When you have a weapon, it becomes an extension of you. You can carry a shield, a staff, wear your armor, and use every tool imaginable to protect yourself, but there is a limit. A sword cannot grab your opponent. A shield can only strike if it is not being used to defend. Armor can aid you for a heavy blow, but that strike will not be true if the one within does not know how to punch."

Magnus took a step back and danced around the court-yard. A dance she'd only seen from him once before. It was a warrior's dance. A mix of the strikes, kicks, and forms he had mastered over the years. As beautiful as it could be fierce in battle.

"My weapon is not simply an extension of me, it is me. I have no armor, so I must fight with more skill than my opponent since each blow could be fatal. I cannot strike at range, so each attack must be precise, and it must be dealt with a purpose. That's what I learned watching those men fight in that ring. What it meant to give my all to every fight — body, blood, and soul."

"Wow," Neoma picked up the practice sword and twirled it around in her hand, "that was a much more interesting story than that awful dribble you spout in the common room."

Magnus laughed, wiping a tear from his eye when he was finished. "The men and women of the guard love my tales. Do not mock me because you fail to spin such entertainment for our comrades."

"They are drunken fools in the light of the moon. Your stories are the most action they'll ever get when they're off duty."

"Come now," Magnus walked towards the den with a chuckle, "we have a long journey ahead of us in the morning. Rest in one of my guest rooms. We'll meet the others at the gates at first light."

Neoma nodded and strode over to place the practice sword back in the basket. She looked down at her hands, still and sturdy as stone. She took a deep breath and clenched her fist.

I'm not alone. Not anymore.

6

Blood of the Crown

The moonlight filled King Mirian's personal quarters with a silvery glow. He peered out the window and looked down at the city he had ruled over for nearly two decades. He loved the kingdom and everything that it stood for. He thought over the decisions he'd made through the years and wondered if he had been on the right path. A knock on the door ripped him from his introspection before he could devise an answer that satisfied him.

"My liege," Erelwyn's voice floated beneath the door, "may I enter?"

"Come in, Erel."

Erelwyn opened the door slowly and stepped through the archway, shutting the door behind him. He dropped on one knee and bowed his head. King Mirian kept his back to the doorway, but the shuffling behind him was all too familiar. He shook his head and sighed.

"You and Magnus can be quite insistent on formalities that I would rather do without."

Erelwyn grit his teeth and a small growl rumbled in his throat. "You are my king. Therefore, I see it only right that I show you the proper respect."

"You are also my brother, Erel." King Mirian turned and walked towards Erelwyn. "Though you are not the son of the previous queen, we are still blood through our father's line. I will not have you bow to me in private as though we are not equals."

Erelwyn nodded to King Mirian and walked past him. He took a seat at the small table nestled in the corner of the room and placed a scroll on the table. King Mirian took a seat opposite him and picked up the message. He read it over twice before rising from his chair and tossing the parchment into the small flames crackling in the fireplace. His face flickered with strange shadows as the paper crumbled to ashes.

"The death of Alandriel was the final straw. I don't care for honeyed words and empty promises," King Mirian whispered into the flames.

"Are you certain it was wise to send that man? Too many words shared over the course of this mission could ruin everything that you have worked for over the last fifteen years, my King."

King Mirian shook his head. "Magnus will either kill him or be killed. It is highly unlikely the Ahndaele woman he trained will allow him to fall. Elias is there to ensure things go as wanted. Whatever he learns about our actions is inconsequential. Magnus is certain to punish Cade for his misdeeds, but no one will forget the last sixteen years. It is his word against my own."

"Then I shall prepare the others to move to their post. The

other captains have kept operations as normal. We're close to recreating what the Mistress of Mercy took with her. I will update you with their progress." Erelwyn began to lean forward, then stopped himself. He walked past King Mirian, placing one hand on his shoulder as he passed by him. Mirian set his hand atop Erelwyn's with a deep sigh. Erelwyn exited the room without another word. King Mirian stood stilL, the warmth of the fire bringing him little comfort.

"Yes," he whispered to himself, "this is the right course of action. Of that I am certain."

7

On the Trail Again

With the rising of the sun, both Magnus's and Neoma's squadrons stood by the city gates, both prepared for the journey ahead. Ten men and women prepared to march into the darkest depths if their captains commanded them to do so. However, Magnus noticed that his squadron seemed far less motivated than Neoma's. They looked to their captain for the strength that they could not find in themselves. She shined before them, while his soldiers only looked to him for orders.

"We're ready to take on whatever beast bares its fangs at us, sir. Just say the—" Boram looked past Magnus and his face twisted into a grimace. "What do you think you're doing here?"

Magnus turned to find Elias walking down the pathway. Elias stood between Magnus and Neoma, meeting the abundance of disgruntled faces with a smug grin.

"Well now, if it isn't Boram Moensteur. I haven't seen you since the academy. Don't tell me," Elias let out a feigned gasp, "are you not happy to see me?"

Boram growled and jerked forward. Magnus placed himself between the two of them and met both of their gazes with a stern scowl. "Both of you cease this childish prattling. King Mirian has placed a shadow within our ranks for this mission. He is an ally, and we shall treat him as such. Am I understood?"

His words were met with dissatisfied grunts and murmurs, but Boram backed down and no one else made any moves towards Elias.

"And you," Magnus looked at Elias. "Do not antagonize my guards. If you must be here, then you will show them the same respect that you offer me."

"Consider it done," Elias replied.

Magnus looked up at Neoma and nodded. Before they had left the villa, they decided that it would be best if she was to lead the march. The association of their targets to Cade was sure to skew his judgement and he refused to endanger his squad with his own quest for revenge. He was also beginning to feel the effects of the alcohol withdrawal and before long he was sure to find himself in a weakened state. His abilities to lead were far too impeded to take the front of such a large group.

The local herbalist provided him with a few herbs to keep the symptoms at bay, but his supply was limited. How long this journey would be was beyond them, but today was the first step. As far as Magnus was concerned, every step towards Grithala was another step towards his daughter.

They traveled at a steady pace due to their numbers. The capital cities in each kingdom were heavily fortified, but the surrounding territories were home to many of the bandit and thief guilds around Aévan. The policing of organized crime in the kingdoms was left to the local guard corps. However, the criminal gangs were often left to their own business unless their crimes became too noticeable.

The guilds who came from No Man's Land were a different story. The bandit guilds from No Man's Land were often referred to as the Murder Guilds by civilians. The members were bloodthirsty and considered savage. Stories reached all corners of the realm about the rampages they left in their wake. None were more feared than the Emerald Blood. Cade rose further than any bandit captain had ever gone from No Man's Land. He brought fear and destruction wherever he went, and his power was so terrifying that Astoria sent a Royal Army detachment after him — an act that was almost unheard of against anything other than enemy detachments from other kingdoms.

Magnus knew full well how ruthless Cade could be. His anger burned deep in the pit of his stomach and he was certain that there was little that could be done to staunch his rage. He was usually a man who preferred to subdue his enemies, but he wondered if he could make the same decision when it came to Cade. *Could I stop myself from taking his life?* The question spun through his mind again and again.

Neoma stood stalwart at the front of the squadrons. She was composed and the air around her burned with her ferocity, but inside her mind was filled with as many questions as Magnus's. She knew she was taking on more than she was sure of, but she refused to back down, to show weakness. Growing up, she was kicked around far too often to bow down to her own shortcomings. Magnus needed her to do this. For her, that was the only motivation she needed.

She had her own power, and she could stand on her own two feet. When she saw him, that is what she was reminded of. When she felt like she had nothing, it was Magnus that gave her the strength she kept locked away. Even if he didn't know it.

She glanced over her shoulder at him. His face was contorted in something like pity and anger. She could only imagine that he was directing that pitiful visage inward. His hands were trembling and sweat was beading down his neck. It pained her, to see a man that she admired so much suffering from his own mistakes. Though his pain was all too real, something she knew she would never fully understand, he descended into habits that could have destroyed him if not for his resilience to live.

Neoma returned her gaze to the forward and continued to lead the march. Every guard walked with purpose and strength. The only one who fell from sight was Elias. He chose to move about the shadows; his presence all but erased from their vision. But he was there, slinking through the darkness at their sides, watching them. He saw the gaze Neoma threw to Magnus. He saw the pain in Magnus's eyes. He saw the fear in Boram's step when his face remained stern.

He saw them all. Still, he remained without expression. He didn't pity them. He did not laugh, nor think them fools. He understood their pain and their worries, but they were beyond his reach. He had one goal and one purpose. He had his blade — murky and hellish though it was — encased in the darkness that bent to his will. He had but one target and for now, that blade stayed hidden in the shadows that clung to their worries, fear, and harrowed nightmares.

* * *

Four days passed before Grithala came into view. Travel through the rolling valleys of Astoria's more rural region was relatively easy with their numbers. They rested every six hours and made camp at sundown. Every night was filled with drink and merriment for those who could handle the release and still be ready to fight if needed in the morning.

Magnus spent every night sharpening his skills before resting beneath the stars. He made a tea from the herbs he'd bought and propped himself wherever he saw fit. Neoma was more confident in her current skill level, but her knowledge of the land troubled her. She studied the maps and charts that she was given every chance she got.

"You look as though you're searching for some forgotten treasure in those lines," he would tease her.

Though she was certain her studying seemed obsessive, she always retorted, "Well one must seek fortune lest they die a guard with little more than a silver coin to their name."

It felt good for both of them to speak without tension or motives unknown. It reminded them of their days together in the Royal Guard before Neoma became a captain. They had spent hours together on stakeouts. Magnus had already lost his family, but he showed more of himself at the time. He hadn't given up hope yet. Now that someone has spotted the Emerald Blood, now that he had some sort of tether to Cade, some of that hope returned and, with it, Magnus.

As usual, it was only Elias who found himself alone when

they made camp. It was his life as a Shadow, a member of the Astorian Spy Corps, that separated him from the rest. Nobody trusted the Spy Corps. They were deemed *sinister* by the Royal Guard and civilians alike. Though the Spy Corps is named as such, their true role was often as killers; assassins that dealt in spilling blood before their enemies were aware they were being stalked. This was seen as shameful for an Ahndaele.

"Warriors don't fight from the shadows. They face their opponents with honor. Something you lack." These words were echoed by every citizen of Astoria.

Shadows, they called them, something made of darkness. That was what Elias was, and he was prepared to be hated for it, or so he thought. Looking out at Magnus and Neoma, he envied them. Even with the fall from grace that Magnus suffered, he was respected, loved, and acknowledged. The Spy Corps was taught to remove emotion from their lives and focus only on the mission. They were told that happiness was only earned by staying alive and doing what needed to be done.

Elias leaned back in the grass on the hilltop and sighed into the night sky. His eyes lingered on a single, brilliant light floating by its lonesome amidst the vast sea of bright stars.

"What am I worried for?" he whispered to himself. "Never forget why they chose you. There is nothing and no one waiting for you to come home. That is why you wield this blade."

He held his hand in front of his face and swirled the shadows around it. The handle of a dagger formed in his palm and before long his fully formed blade danced between his fingertips. He stared at the jagged edges of his dagger and the demonic form it took on when it was first given to him. The red that ran the length of the blade was so eerie, even to him, that he wasn't surprised when people shuddered at the sight of it. The curved handle gave the entire weapon the visage of some venomous snake ready to strike at any moment.

"So that's one of the infamous *Sygerths* carried by the Shadows?" Magnus stood next to Elias with a raised brow.

Elias sat up and held the blade out in front of him. "Yes. The *Sygerth* is the weapon we are given when they pick us from the academy. I am surprised you know its true name. Most call it by its more commonly known moniker — the Hell Blade."

Elias twirled it around once more before flinging it into the ground. The dagger vanished in a puff of smoke and shadow as it pierced the earth. Magnus watched the wispy tendrils fade into the night before sitting next to Elias.

"Tomorrow we reach Grithala. I imagine meeting the contact will not be so simple as walking up and exchanging greetings."

"Of that, you can be certain," Elias replied, "but do not concern yourself with the means of our contact. I would much prefer you focus on steadying yourself, *jyulmain*. If things go sideways, I will prefer we all make it back alive."

"Careful, Elias. Someone might think you care about other people." Magnus stood from the ground and extended his hand towards Elias. "Fine, I will leave the point of contact in your capable hands. For what it's worth, I am glad that you're here. You're strong. Even if our own fear you, we may need that strength."

Elias's eyes fell on Magnus's hand, hanging in the air between them. His right arm twitched but remained at his side. He looked up at Magnus and returned his gesture with a simple nod. Magnus retracted his hand and smirked before walking back over to Neoma.

"So, what did he say?" Neoma asked upon Magnus's return.

"Nothing of interest. He shall handle point of contact. He did not divulge the means of the situation."

"Are you sure you trust him to do so?" Neoma looked over at Magnus, her finger tapping rapidly against her knee. "I know that you have known him for quite some time, but he is still one of them."

"Do not worry, Neoma. He may be a Shadow, but I do trust Elias. He is far more honest than anyone of us. Sometimes much more so than necessary. A stubborn man for sure, but one who stands by his word. If he says he will handle it, I believe he will. We just have to back him up if something goes wrong."

Neoma nodded and took a sip of her ale. "Tomorrow feels as though things will certainly change."

"Well, you are the one with the foresight. How do you feel that change will play out?"

"Quiet yourself. You know that's not how my sight works. This vision is not of my eye. It is more of a feeling. Whether that feeling is good or bad... only the hours will tell."

"We may be on in years, but we are far too young to let a night such as this pass us by with something so dull as philosophy. Come," Magnus stood and held his hand out to her, "let us gather our brothers and sisters. I have a story or two I can tell."

8

Savages Among Men

Grithala was bustling with preparations for the Harvest Festival. Merchants and traders raced through the stone streets of the township with carts loaded with crops, goods, and trinkets from all over. Though Grithala was small, this was the one time of year when the entire town would be full of travelers from the neighboring towns and nearby cities. The festival brought joy to many and fortune to the lucky few who prepared the best wares before the day came around.

Wulthuin, a rather boisterous and plump geezer, from the neighboring town of Falswain, dragged his cart around every inch of the city to find his perfect location to set up his stand. He had never before made it to the festival over the years that he had opened his bakery in his hometown, but this year he was certain that he would finally make enough money to send his son to the Ahndaele Academy in Astoria.

"That boy needs a good kick in the ass, Uyala," Wulthuin said to his wife.

"Sweetheart, he wants to be an explorer. He says it's his

dream to chart out the unexplored regions of No Man's Land. I think it's a wonderful goal."

"Wonderful?" The vein in his head looked as though it were about to burst through his skin. "That boy would be torn to pieces by one of them murder guilds or eaten alive by a lurker out in them parts. There's a reason them lands ain't been charted. The beasts are as dangerous as the people!"

He whipped his head around to face his wife and failed to see the man walking past them. He bumped right into him, feeling as though he'd collided with a brick wall. He fell backward, colliding with the edge of his cart and howling in pain.

"Dammit all!" he screamed out. "Why don't you watch where yer going, you big oaf. Yer as solid as a rock."

Cade turned to face the man who collided with him and leaned down with a toothy grin. He held his hand out for the man and looked into his eyes with a menacing glare.

"My apologies, sir. I suppose I should be more careful next time. I would hate for someone to get injured on my account."

The man smacked away Cade's hand and attempted to hoist himself up from the ground by his cart. The Emerald Blood members behind Cade laughed at the sight of the round man struggling to lift himself from the ground. Cade shot them a nasty glance and their chuckling ceased in an instant. He leaned forward and extended another helping hand to Wulthuin.

Wulthuin swatted his hand again and continued to lift himself up. "I don't need yer damn help. Leave me be."

"As you wish. Though I do feel bad. Perhaps there is something I could do for you in return. I couldn't help but overhear your conversation. If your son dreams of adventuring out into the Wildlands, I would be happy to tell you everything I know of the area."

"The Wildlands, eh?" Wulthuin muttered, finally on his feet. "Ain't that what them savages call it? The ones who grew up out there in No Man's Land? You can't be one of them. You talk too proper and all."

"Indeed, I was born in the Wildlands. Though my speech is something of an acquired skill. However, if I were you, I wouldn't call them savages. I hear they hate the term."

Behind Cade, the other members of the Emerald Blood looked on at Wulthuin with daggers in their eyes. Uyala shuddered at the sight of their hateful gaze. She could see by the scarring on their exposed skin that they were likely the very same people that Cade spoke of. The raised skin in the shape of intricate tribal tattoos identified them as natives of the Wildlands, but even with all of their terrifying presence, Wulthuin seemed to not notice any of it.

"Well perhaps if they were more like us civilized folk, then we wouldn't call them savages. I'm just saying, if they don't like it, then they should learn."

The corners of Cade's twisted smile lifted higher, giving his face the appearance of a wolf baring its teeth at its prey. "What is your definition of 'civilized' if I may ask? Is it the way you speak in such a hateful manner against people you know nothing of? Is it perhaps the control you all seem to love placing on those you call loved ones? Or perhaps it's the way you lot seem to enjoy fattening yourselves up... like pigs to the slaughter."

"Well, now who do you think you—"

"Wulthuin, let's just leave," Uyala interjected.

Cade glanced over at her, acknowledging her presence for the first time. He was baffled at the sight of her standing next to the boorish creature she called a husband. Compared to him, she was a welcome sight. Her curvaceous figure was framed well by her waist-length crimson hair. Her vibrant blue eyes were only made more astonishing against the paleness of her skin that was dotted with small brown freckles. He gave her a disingenuous smile and met her gaze.

"No. Please don't worry. *You* are in no danger here. I simply wish to make your husband understand that his idea of civilized life is not quite so perfect."

"What do you know, boy? If you are one of them savages, then you ain't nothing but a fraud talking like you some type of noble," Wulthuin spat at Cade.

"What I know," Cade grabbed a fistful of Wulthuin's shirt and lifted him a foot off the ground, "is that while your people murder, steal, and rape countless numbers of your own civilians, my people are called savages; the people who only wish to survive out there in the land your rich kings and nobles deemed too dangerous to travel. But you see, I'm not like them. No, I'm not one of the good ones. I'm one of the bad ones. A true savage, just like you."

Uyala screamed in horror at the sight of Wulthuin being lifted as though he was little more than a sack of potatoes. Cade brought his face closer to Wulthuin's and snarled. Wulthuin cried out in fear, looking around as best he could for someone to step in and help him. The guards walking the streets nearby refused to even turn their heads in the direction of the commotion — walking past them as though there was nothing to be seen nor heard.

"Never forget, old man, who the true savages are. It isn't them. It's you and I. Us and the rest of your so-called civilized people are the real monsters. Because even with all my love for the people in the Wildlands, I'd sooner turn them into corpses for my own profit. So, imagine what I would do to a pig like you."

Cade released Wulthuin's shirt and let him fall to the ground with a loud *plop* on the stone below him. Cade turned to Uyala and a crooked grin spread across his face.

"Since I'm feeling generous during such a wonderful festival such as this, I'll make you a deal, pig. Give your delicious looking wife to me, and I'll let you leave this town with your life. Sound fair?"

Wulthuin nodded his head vigorously, backing towards his cart with sweat dripping down his face and neck and fear widening his eyes.

Cade laughed and shook his head. "What a pathetic excuse for a man. Well, it seems you belong to me know, gorgeous."

He grabbed Uyala's arm and led her away from Wulthuin. He did not move — she did not fight. Neither uttered a word, but tears streamed down Wulthuin's face. Uyala's expression was blank. She couldn't believe how quickly her husband agreed to trade her off to save his own skin. In an instant, he was dead to her.

"Like I said," Cade leaned down and whispered into her ear, "civilized men are little more than beasts — willing to do whatever it takes to save themselves."

"Do what you want with me, just please, tell my son I love him," Uyala murmured.

"Please, you're free to tell him yourself. I have no intention of keeping you from him. We shall retrieve him on our journey home. I intend to keep my promise. Your son will realize his dream. On that, you have my word."

Cade released her arm and continued to walk forward. Uyala swallowed the lump in her throat and walked behind him. Without turning, Cade spoke to the other members of the Emerald Blood that followed behind her.

"I don't expect the pig to stay in town for the festival. The moment he crosses the border, kill him."

9

The Crumbling Path

Magnus, Neoma, Elias, and the two squadrons set out at first light. The trembling in Magnus's hands was only exacerbated by the closing distance between him and the Emerald Blood.

The rolling hillsides they had traveled for the last few days gave way to craggy mountain slopes. Elias traversed the terrain with ease — disappearing and reappearing in a puff of shadow and smoke. Rhaste, a guardswoman in Neoma's squadron, walked up front with the two captains. Her ability to manipulate earth helped them cover the more difficult land, but the usage had to be kept to a minimum the closer they came to Grithala. Magnus watched her shift the heavy stones with ease and couldn't help but be impressed.

"With such an ability, I'd have thought you'd be placed with the Royal Army. Why are you only a guard?" he asked.

"My family, sir. My mother needed me in the city to help care for my younger brother. She's sick and can only do so much. I always wanted to fight, so I went to the Academy, but when it came time to choose, I decided to stay close by."

"That's admirable. Very admirable. Always remember that as a warrior. Our first job, above all else, is to protect those we love. The way we do that may vary, but it is always our first priority."

"Aye, sir," Rhaste replied. "I would give my life for my kingdom, but there are times I do fear that the price of my life, is theirs."

"Good. Fear is not a weakness of the strong, it is what keeps them alive. No sword shall strike your back if you remain vigilant and cautious. Do your utmost to return home to your mother and younger brother. I should like to meet them. Tell your brother stories of his brave older sister."

A wide smile crossed Rhaste's face. Magnus could see the toll this mountainside was taking on her. With a power like his own, he often forgot the physical limitations of other abilities. Even if she did not have to pick every stone up into her arms, she still moved them by the strength of her will and that takes a toll on one's stamina.

"We're nearly there. I can see the town line across the next valley," Elias called from a few meters above.

The announcement filled everyone with a renewed sense of energy. They pressed on, skimming the side of the mountain with relative ease. However, the ledges became thinner and the slopes steepened the further they pushed on. With only a few meters to go, there was nearly no space for them to walk on, and they were in sight of the city. Having Rhaste reform the side of the mountain risked giving away their position.

"Perhaps instead of a full path, I could create small footholds along the edge. It should be enough to get one person across at a time," Rhaste suggested.

"Okay, let's go slow and steady. Rhaste, lead the way," Neoma said.

With a small nod, Rhaste turned and set to work making the footholds. Each one was big enough to take one step at a time. Their pace slowed the closer they go to their destination. Rhaste's breathing was heavy and her face and neck were soaked in sweat. She reached out and another foothold protruded from the mountainside, but Magnus could see that it was significantly thinner than the others.

He reached forward and called out. "Rhaste wait!"

Rhaste hesitated, but her foot was already on the thin foothold. It snapped underneath her weight. She fell forward. Her head collided with the side of the mountain, knocking her unconscious as she fell further down.

A loud *crack* behind them tossed Magnus's head to the side. Boram leapt from his foothold and dove down towards Rhaste. Everyone looked on in horror as the two plummeted towards certain death. Boram fell faster, gaining more and more on Rhaste's unconscious body. When he was close enough to reach out to her, he grabbed her arm and turned his other arm to steel, jamming it into the mountainside far enough to stop their fall. with a loud *pop* Rhaste's arm dislocated from her shoulder, but Boram managed to keep them hanging from the side of the mountain.

He looked around and found a cliff big enough to hold both of them. He swung her limp body back and forth, tossing her to the cliffside before turning his other arm and climbing that way.

"Alright, I'm done playing hero for the day!" Boram yelled up to the others. "Someone come down and save our asses!"

Every member of the squadrons, including Magnus and Neoma, couldn't help but let out a nervous chorus of laughter. For a moment, time had stopped, and in a long, drawn out instant, Boram brought everything back.

The rest of them put their heads together, and their powers, and figured out a way to get the rest of them across with no further incidents. After another hour, the rest of them had scaled the side of the mountain safely.

"Now, how do we get Boram and Rhaste up here?" One of the other guardsmen asked.

In an answer to his question, Elias appeared next to them with Rhaste in his arms. He laid her at Neoma's feet and straightened her out with care.

"Elias, tha—" Before Neoma could get the words out he was gone again.

A moment later he reappeared with a disgruntled Boram. Boram pushed away from him and stomped over to his squadron.

"Thanks for the save. I owe you one, Shadow." He turned with a grimace. "I still don't trust ya though."

Elias clicked his tongue and walked over to where he'd laid Rhaste's limp body at Neoma's feet. "Hold her for me, will ya?"

Neoma nodded and leaned down to help him. He gripped her arm and popped it back in place, but he could see that it was far from healed. A swirl of shadows appeared next to him.

He reached his hand in and pulled a length of cloth from it. He went to work wrapping her arm in a sling and setting it across her torso. He reached his hand in again and grabbed a small glass bottle with a silvery liquid inside. He uncapped it and leaned it towards Rhaste's mouth.

"Ay! What's that you're tryna give her? Better not be some kind of poison. This ain't no time for mercy killin'," Boram shouted from behind Elias.

"It's a tonic, fool. I always keep a few from the apothecary. It should speed up her healing and reduce the pain. She's not long for this world if the wound on her head remains open."

He tipped the bottle into her mouth, lifted her head, and helped her get the tonic down her throat. Almost instantly, the wound began to close, and her eyes blinked open.

"Wh... what happened?" Rhaste whispered.

"Your wings were clipped, little bird. You'll be alright now," Elias replied. "You won't be of much use as a fighter for the rest of this journey. I suggest you rest. We'll get you to a medic in Grithala as soon as possible."

"No," Rhaste placed her good hand on the ground and pushed herself up. "My place is here with the rest of you."

Magnus walked forward and placed his hand Rhaste's sling. "He's right. I admire your spirit, but you have those who you wish to return to back home. We know not what we will face on the other side of this valley."

"After some time, I will be able to use my abilities again. I assure you I am still of use."

Magnus and Elias glanced over to Neoma. She looked between Rhaste and the rest of the guards looking on with anticipation. She couldn't help but take in the mix of admiration and worry on their faces. As the leader, she knew her decision must only depend on the best interest of the mission, but she also knew the place Rhaste now stood. She wanted to more than anything to prove that she could do this for herself. Returning home without completing the mission is a blow to a warrior's pride beyond many others.

Neoma shut her eyes and took a deep breath. "I will allow you to continue with us, but if things take a turn for the worst, your role is support. Use your abilities to create defensive barriers and protect your brothers and sisters in arms. Is that understood?"

Rhaste met Neoma's stern gaze and nodded. The other squad members celebrated her presence. Neoma looked over at Magnus and wondered if she had made the right choice. He understood the uncertainty in her eyes. He met her fears with a soft smile. He was certain she was far more of a leader than he was. She understood the feelings of her subordinates and came up with an appropriate plan of action in mere seconds. He was sure he would have ordered her home and likely ruined the morale of the entire squadron in an instant. Even after such a perilous event, with her method, they seemed more invigorated than before. He hadn't taught her this, and now he was learning from her.

"Let's continue forward. Elias you s—" Neoma turned to where the shadow once stood, but he had already vanished from sight.

Elias watched their merriment from inside his own darkness. They would likely see the town line once they turned. He wasn't needed to give them direction. As sure as his thought, they turned and marched forward. There was only half a day left until they reached their destination. They were to meet the scout when the sun began to set. Despite their setbacks, they were on time, but Elias couldn't shake the feeling of unease. Every step they took made him glance over his shoulder more and more often. Something other than the wind was at their backs, and he wasn't sure his blade would be enough to cull this threat.

10

Legend of the Silver Moon

The rest of their journey across the valley was calm. Magnus walked at the head of the group with Neoma, but his step was backward. True to himself, he faced the guards that should have been at his back and wove one of his famous tales to take their minds off the events to come.

"This is one tale that is sure to excite any man or woman!" he began. "The final ride of the Silver Moon. The greatest battalion ever known in Astoria."

"You didn't ride with the Silver Moon, you fool," Neoma chuckled. "You couldn't have been more than a pup when they vanished."

The rest of the squadrons joined in her laughter.

"Ay, she's right, sir," Boram joined in. "I might love your stories, but even this one seems a bit too farfetched."

"No, no. You might be right that I was not one of them. Ay, I was but a pup, but I was with them, nonetheless. Even if they were unaware of that fact when we ventured beyond the city walls."

Neoma sputtered and coughed at his words. She looked at him in disbelief and he met her shock with a chest-pounding laugh.

"Yes, I snuck upon the caravan that the Silver Moon rode out with on their final journey. For you see, my father, Cygnus, was the commander of the Silver Moon. I snuck into his storage chest before he loaded it into the caravan, and I set out with the legendary battalion of the Astoria Royal Army."

Everyone fell quiet. Some had their jaws dropped in shock and awe. Neoma was the only one who looked at him as though he were a bigger fool than she previously thought. She was used to the antics of the drunken master she's come to admire, but something as reckless as sneaking off with a Royal Army battalion was a death wish for a child.

"What kind of stupid child goes off alone to sneak out with a Royal Army caravan?" she asked.

"Now who said I was alone?"

"Don't tell me..."

"Ah yes, you are aware of my childhood best friend. King Mirian himself, though at the time he was the third prince. Both of us slipped into the caravan that day. We wanted nothing more than a life of adventure at the prime of our tenth year. His father commanded the battalion to intercept a Theldenian force twice their number near the valleys below Wynder Peak. I was always interested in the ways of the Ahndaele. I wanted to see the mightiest warriors in our kingdom in action, not just hear stories."

Every eye in the group was on him. Stories of the Silver

Moon were few and far between in the kingdom. They were a sort of legend that seemed cursed to speak about. Even when they were still around, no one knew who they were. Their names were left out of records and the only proof of their existence was their insignia and the fear in the few enemies who managed to escape with their lives. To find out that someone so close to them was related to a member of the fabled battalion was more than most of them could have ever hoped for.

"I heard whispers of the commander when I was a lad," Boram spoke up. "What kind of Ahndaele was he? Nobody ever seemed to know."

"He was an Ahndaele Fey, like your survivor Rhaste here," Magnus answered. "His element was the wind. When I was a boy, he would lift me upon his back and we would soar over the forest near Crowind."

Magnus's words faltered for a moment. The mention of Crowind reminded him why he brought Alandriel there. He shook away the foul mood creeping on him and went back to his story.

"So, we traveled in the chest for a full day before we made our presence known. Though perhaps I should say before we were discovered. My father called for his trunk and inside he found his darling, stupid son." He made a grand gesture with his hand. "He was furious, but even the other battalion leaders laughed at the explanation Mirian and I gave them. They worried more about having the prince along than me. Nevertheless, it was too late for them to return us to the kingdom. They would have had to send too many members to escort the prince back and the Theldenian forces were advancing further with every passing day."

"The mission doesn't sound like anything near their toughest adventures from the stories heard in the city. What happened to them?" Rhaste asked.

"The thing is, even I don't know. We traveled for a week, learning to hunt beasts and fend for ourselves off the land along the way. It was a great adventure. However, when the battalion neared the final location where they were meant to intercept the enemy, Mirian and I were hidden away in a nearby village. We were only a few kilometers off, but for two long nights, we heard not a clash of steel or cry for battle. The peaks and valleys were quiet and calm. Eventually, we grew curious and ventured from our safe lodgings to the place where the battle should have taken place."

"What did you find?"

"Bodies. Yet none bore the crest of the Silver Moon. The Theldenian forces, likely all of them, lay dead in the valley. Waves of red grass swayed in the winds as though the sight were nothing out of the norm. There were no other bodies, no blades nor arrows in that valley. Just a sea of slaughtered men and women. Except for one. In the center of that field was one man, still breathing, leaning against the hilt of his blade as it was jammed into the ground."

"Was it your father, sir?" The guards leaned forward, waiting for the revelation.

"No, it was another name that many of you likely do remember, though his involvement in this event was largely hidden. The legendary Ahndaele Erelis Tyriol. The man who stood above the entire Royal Army until he drew his last breath."

"Magister Erelwyn's father?" Neoma asked.

"The very same. He was only a captain at the time, but he was out in the area on a personal surveying mission when he stumbled upon the Theldenian. At least, that's the story we were told. The story goes when he was discovered they tried to capture him. He disarmed one of the soldiers and for three days he fought them singlehandedly. They say he killed one thousand men that day. From then on, they called him the one-man army."

"Don't get me wrong, that's all well and good, sir. I'm incredibly impressed if the story is true, but what of the Silver Moon? If he was the one who took out the enemy forces, where was your father and his men?"

"Master Erelis was nearing unconsciousness when we found him — still upright by sheer force of will. Mirian and I dragged him back to the cabin that we'd been hiding in and we stayed with him until he was able to pull himself from the bed. In his haze, he spoke of shadows and beasts. He whispered the names of things that prowl in the darkness, but not once, even when he was conscious, could he say that he saw my father's battalion. The Silver Moon was gone that day and not one person could explain why. Not one person could find a trace of their steps or a scrap of their presence. They became a story — legend."

Magnus turned around and looked off into the distance. He thought of his final memories with his father, hunting boar and having his first taste of ale. He knew the story he told was true, at least to the parts of it he'd seen with his own eyes, but he had to admit that it sounded beyond reality.

"Well, what kind of story is that!" Boram yelled. "I thought the Silver Moon must have gone down in a blaze of glory! You tellin' me they just soddin' vanished without a trace? That's fuckin' horrifying!"

Everyone laughed at his words. Boram's outrage warmed their chilled hearts and minds. The story horrified them, but it also intrigued them. Thoughts of the mysterious disappearance swirled in their minds.

"You're missing the point there, Boram," Magnus called back.

"And what is that point, eh?"

Elias appeared out of a swirl of shadows a few feet in front of them. "The point is, even after they vanished, they are remembered for the strength and ferocity of their previous deeds. Even though almost no one knows their names, they're still admired throughout nearly every household that heard whispers of their legends. So do not fret what comes after. Remember what you've done, and you will always be remembered as a warrior."

"Well, perhaps that's what I should've planned to say."

"Oh, and what were you going to say?" Neoma asked.

"Well, I—" Magnus stammered.

Elias held his hand up and hissed. "We've no time. We're here and so is he."

All eyes glanced around. They'd been so engrossed in the tale that they had not realized they had reached the southern checkpoint. Magnus and Neoma looked around for the scout, but no one was there except for them.

"Silhouettes and honey," a voice whispered from the air.

"A hunter's greatest weapons," Elias responded.

Upon his response, a figure shimmered in front of them and a Grithalan scout appeared in the once unoccupied space.

He was young, no more than twenty years, and his armor shifted on his body as he moved. He lurched forward in an awkward, half-hearted bow. Magnus and Neoma crossed an arm across their chests and saluted the ragged scout.

The young boy stayed in the bowed position for far longer than one would ever deem necessary. Magnus sensed an immense fear from him, but it didn't seem to be directed towards them.

"Stand straight boy and give us the information," Elias ordered.

The boy jumped and stumbled forward. He steadied himself and looked up at the three stern faces before him and jammed his hand into the pack hanging off his waist. His hands trembled as he handed Elias the sealed scroll.

"He-here it is, sir," he stammered.

"Why are you so nervous, scout?" Neoma asked with a raised brow.

Magnus had already gone to work and opened the scroll. His eyes poured over the page and the further he read, the darker his eyes seemed to become.

"I see. So that's what you saw in their encampment."Elias handed the scroll to Neoma.

"So, there's a witch with them. Are you certain it was an actual witch?" she asked the scout.

"Y-yes ma'am," he said, "I saw three of her talents for myself. Fire, water, and earth. She might have more, but I was too scared to stay any longer."

The three of them bit their lips in frustration. Ahndaele Fey were difficult enough to combat. Their manipulative abilities were revered on a battlefield for their strength, but even they were limited to one. A witch had multiple talents, and one that had already mastered three was sure to hold the same advantage as thirty extra men in their encampment. Suddenly their numbers felt small compared to the power of their enemy.

"The presence of the witch doesn't change the mission." Neoma turned and faced the squadrons. "Are any of you deterred now that we know they have a witch among them? Are any of you ready to give up on our mission?"

"NO!"

"That's what I thought. So, we continue as planned. We now know that they set up camp in a mountain cave on the north side of the township. We'll devise a plan of action and likely ambush them when night falls. For now, let's set up camp ourselves and prepare for the battle to come."

The soldiers roared in agreement and spread out to set up their camp. The scout gave another clumsy bow and vanished into thin air once more.

"An ambush at night? Careful, Captain. Tactics like that might make people believe you're more like the Spy Corps than you think." Elias smirked.

"I don't plan to stab a man in the back in the comfort of his own home. The ambush is to corner them and gain the advantage. I am no assassin. I will face my enemy head-on." Neoma stomped off towards the center of the sprouting camp.

"Perhaps," Elias whispered, "but I won't give the witch such luxuries."

11

A Message Most Dire

Mirian stood in his bedroom and let out a deep sigh. He had spent the majority of his day meeting with nobles about their grievances. His energy was all but depleted and he was thankful for a moment of peace. He set to work unlatching his armor, placing it on the stand in the corner of the room. He stripped the rest of his clothes off and opened his armoire to decide on his evening wear.

"If it weren't for our children joining us for dinner, I might ask that you remain as you are," Teferi whispered, her hands running the length of his back.

Mirian smiled and chuckled. "My dear wife, your words are as liberated as they were when we were teens."

"Oh, should I stop then?" she asked with sarcasm painting her tone. "I can become your prim and proper lady of the court at all times."

Mirian laughed louder this time. He turned and wrapped his arms around his wife. He looked into his queen's eyes and felt himself getting lost in the beautiful honey-brown of her irises. She smiled wide at him and he couldn't help but match her vibrance.

"I shun the thought of you being anyone but yourself." He pressed his lips against hers and felt himself renewed.

"Yes, well you would think someone who appreciates me that much would do something with that unruly hair I have complained about so often."

"I'll have you know I like my long hair. I think it makes me look more majestic as a ruler."

"Majestic is for horses, my dear." She kissed him once more and turned towards the door.

"Are you saying that I'm not a stallion?"

Teferi laughed and waved his joke off. "Hush now and hurry downstairs. Yuru has prepared a wonderful dinner for us tonight and our daughter will be in attendance."

She walked out the door and it shut with a soft *thud* behind her. Mirian turned towards the mirror and ran his hand through his hair. It had grown nearly a foot longer since the last time he had it trimmed. Now that it had fallen well past his shoulders, he reminded himself so much of his father that it was haunting to see his face in the mirror. He continued to study himself in the mirror and thought back on every scar covering the length of his torso and limbs. Every battle still fresh in his mind.

"I am king now," he whispered to himself. "The time for me to wield a blade has long passed."

He sighed and grabbed one of the garments hanging in the armoire without thinking too long about it now. Within minutes he was dressed and headed to the dining room to be with his family. The halls of the castle were still foreign to him, even after decades of living here. He spent so much time out-side of the walls of his home when he was a boy, he still strug-gled to find some of the many rooms in the vast space.

He sauntered through every winding hall until he found himself in the large dining room where everyone had already been seated. He looked over the room and admired the family that waited for him to arrive.

"I thought we might starve before you showed," his daugh-ter, Talia jested as he approached her.

"My apologies, dear. Your mother made such a fuss about my hair again that I contemplated taking a knife to it before I came down." He leaned down and kissed her forehead.

"Yet the mane remains." A crooked smile crossed Teferi's face.

"You're not going to make me cut my hair, are you Mother?" Alluran asked with a hint of worry in his voice.

Teferi giggled and placed her hand on top of Alluran's. "My sweet boy, you can wear your hair as long as you wish. Let no one tell you otherwise."

Alluran smiled and nodded at his mother. Mirian looked over at his son and realized just how much he looked like the two of them. His son's hair was the same as his own, wavy, dark, and without limit to its length. However, he had his mother's features and sandy skin. He was truly the best of both of them in his appearance.

"Well, now that I am here, let us dig in." Mirian clapped his hands together and started into his chair.

The door to the dining room opened and Erelwyn shuffled in. He walked toward the head of the table and bowed to Mirian.

"My Lord," he said, "my queen."

"Uncle Erel, please, join us," Talia said.

Erelwyn walked over to her and kissed her hand with a small bow of his head. "I would sweetheart, but unfortunately I'm here at the moment on business. My Lord, I must speak of an urgent matter."

"Must it be now Erel? I've only just sat down."

"I do apologize, my Lord. I promise to be quick."

"Fine." Mirian stood from his chair. "Just stop calling me your Lord. Mirian is fine. It is only family present."

Erel nodded and gestured towards the door. Mirian kissed Teferi's hand and turned to walk out of the room. Erel followed close behind him, turning to bow to everyone else before shutting the door behind him.

In the hallway, he peered around the corner before turning to speak to Mirian. "I received a crow some moments ago. It seems they've reached Grithala and made contact with the scout. However, the news is quite troubling."

"What have they said?"

"It seems there is a witch amongst the Emerald Blood. She has three confirmed talents, based on the scout's information."

Mirian bit his lip and kicked his heel into the stone floor. "Damn! This might be beyond the scope of members of the Royal Guard."

"Sir, I fear the ramifications run deeper than that."

"You're right. Either he had the ridiculous luck of stumbling upon a witch..."

"Or he recovered the serum from Alandriel after all. In

which case, we have no idea if this witch is the only one among them," Erelwyn added.

"Send a crow to Grithala immediately. Tell Magnus's squad to fall back and await further orders. We may need to send more Ahndaele Fey to them in order to combat her power."

"Father?" Talia stood behind them with a worried look on her face.

"Talia, dear, when did you get here?" Mirian asked.

"I heard what you said. Send me. I can assist Uncle Magnus with my lightning ability."

Mirian wrapped his arms around Talia. He pulled back and gave her a caring smile, placing his hand on her cheek.

"Sweetheart you are still in the Academy. When you have been granted the status of Ahndaele, then these kinds of battles will be yours to fight, but today is not that day."

"But Father I—"

"Hush now. I will hear no more of this. Join your mother and brother in the dining room. I will return shortly."

Talia hung her head and turned back towards the door. "Yes, Father."

"Talia, speak of this to no one. If the sighting of a witch in enemy hands got out, things could become very dangerous in the city."

Talia nodded and went back into the dining room. Mirian let out a deep sigh and locked eyes with Erelwyn.

"Send the message. We'll form another squadron at first light and send them out before midday."

"Yes, my Lord." Erelwyn bowed and turned down the hall.

"Dammit, Erel. What did I say?" Mirian growled before turning back and heading into the dining room.

12

Alone

The squadron encampment was lively with anticipation. The Grithalan scout returned after the camp was set up with meats and vegetables from the city. The squadrons filled their stomach with the premium stock he provided and laughed around the fires dotted around the grounds.

Magnus, Neoma, and Elias left the others to their own devices and set up their own area off the side of the camp. They watched their guards enjoy the merriment before battle. Their faces were full of smiles, but the tradition of celebration before battle was one of grim cynicism for Astorians. The indulgence of pleasure when one couldn't be certain they could do so after lacked the optimism many hoped for.

"We leave in a few short hours. Hopefully, Boram does not find himself piss drunk in a ditch by that time," Magnus said.

Boram spun one of the other female guards around in the center of the camp with surprising grace. He was brutish at times, but the other guards fed off his energy. Magnus and Elias were well aware that he was the illegitimate son of a noble and his consort, but that never seemed to dampen Boram's effervescence. He was the ideal guard in many ways, but a lech in many others.

"Every one of them has come a long way since they joined the guard, haven't they?" Neoma asked.

"Indeed. I must say I am quite proud of them. They've seen horrendous things in the city, but none of them ever seem to be down on themselves. Even now, as we walk into the maw of the beast, they shine."

"They would be fools not to enjoy this night. As far as I am concerned, it will likely be their last for many of them," Elias muttered.

Magnus and Neoma shook their heads at him. Elias watched their disapproving gestures and shrugged, throwing back a mouthful of his ale.

"Elias, what is it that makes you such an angry man? I know this world is unjust, but celebration should find a healthy mix with disaster." Neoma leaned forward as she spoke. She was a lightweight at best when it came to spirits and ale. One or two glasses eased the tension she packed in her shoulders, but more than that and she became forthright with the most presumptuous statements. Magnus almost admired her tolerance. It was a testament to her aversion to the substance outside of special celebration.

"I believe what she means to ask is why you do not try and enjoy more moments. You often seem as though you prefer to be alone. I know the Spy Corps is not looked upon favorably, but I imagine even amongst the Corps you should be able to find acquaintances," Magnus added.

"Neither of you knows, do you?" Elias looked over their

confused faces. "Do you have any idea how they recruit men and women from the Academy for the Spy Corps?"

Neoma shook her head. "I thought it was a choice given to you during selection meetings. Only given to those with an aptitude for your unique brand of engagement."

"Far from it. One who is being recruited for the Spy Corps is approached from the moment they apply at the Academy. We aren't given a choice. We aren't given options. We are told that it is the Corps, or we can leave the Academy before we step foot over the threshold."

"I don't understand. Why did they approach you? How do they decide?" Magnus asked.

"There are two prerequisites for being chosen for the Corps. That's the part they don't tell you. The reason we are chosen. The first is the murder of someone close to you."

"Murder?" Neoma whispered.

"Yes, murder. Death alone is not enough. They want someone who can blame another for a death they have endured. They believe it breeds anger. With that anger, we are able to utilize the *Sygerth*. It is first manifested by negative emotions. That is the power given to us."

"Who did you lose?" Neoma asked.

Elias looked up at her, then back at the fire. "The second requirement is to be alone. To have nothing and no one to care for you. Whether it is in death or the exile of those close to you, all members of the Spy Corps are ensured to have no family or friends to speak of. This allows us to become what others call us. We become Shadows. With no one looking for us, we are given the chance to move as they command and do what they need us to without conscience and without difficulty."

Neoma stared at Elias, looking for some sort of emotion on his face, but he was unmoved by his own words. His expression did not so much as twitch as he addressed his circumstances. *Would I have been a Shadow too?* she thought to herself.

"I don't understand, Elias. When we were in the Academy, you could have made many friends, but you kept everyone at arm's length. Was it because they'd already approached you? Would it have been so wrong to make a friend or two after accepting their agreement?" Magnus asked.

"You don't get it. Someone like me, who wanted nothing more than to disappear... I found it easy to push people away. It was easier than risking their deaths as well. When everyone around you meets some ill fate, you don't care to make friends. So, perhaps I could have been like you. You were the popular acolyte. The one the others gathered around just to hear you weave ridiculous stories of grandeur. You failed most of the exams, but you excelled at life. I was the opposite. I had nothing but my blade to direct my feelings. That is why I found solace in solitude. It was easier than caring for others when I was sure to lose them."

Neoma jolted up from her seat. She stomped her foot in front of Elias. Her face was contorted in a displeasing mix of anger and pity.

"Your lips move, your eyes show that you hold a heavy heart within your chest, but your words are filled with only half-truths." She stood in front of him with a pointed glare. "I saw you today. You looked upon Rhaste as though your heart would have broken if she were to die. You cannot stop yourself from caring about others. That is a lie we tell ourselves when we are alone and do not believe for a moment that it is for others. We tell ourselves that it is better for others if we stay away, but it is only easier for you. For the one who tells themselves that lie again and again until they fool themselves into believing it."

"What would you know of how I feel, girl? You who is beloved by the kingdom?" Elias spat.

"Because I was you!" Her voice had grown louder. "I grew up in an orphanage with nothing. My mother was killed by some petty thief who wanted her jewelry, and my father drank himself off the top of a cliff."

"Is that so? I cannot say I am sorry for my words, but I do apologize. If that is true, then why were you not recruited? What allowed you to escape the tendrils of the Corps?"

"It was Yeseni, wasn't it?" Magnus asked.

"You remembered." Neoma looked at Magnus wide-eyed.

"Yes, you spoke of her so dearly, I could not forget the name if I tried."

"Who is this person you speak of?" Elias asked.

"She was my only friend. I was prepared to take my life in the orphanage. I thought I had nothing left. Suddenly, this refugee girl from No Man's Land was brought into the orphanage. I hadn't spoken to any of the other children before that day, but she just walked over to me. She handed me a small doll that she had brought with her, and she just smiled. It reminded me of my mother. Just for a moment, I wanted to live."

"You were truly blessed by the ancestors for that moment,"

Elias said, "In truth, I may seem heartless, but even I am not blind to the connections between others. Many of those intrepid young fools dancing about the camp would have different lives if they did not have a leader such as you. Even Magnus here—"

Neoma's eye glowed a bright blue and she gasped. "Elias, duck!"

In the instant the words escaped her lips, an arrow zipped past her head and planted itself in Elias's stomach. He disappeared in a puff of shadows and smoke. The sound of a battle horn rang out and the air around them shook as dozens of bandits clad in black and green armor and robes surrounded them.

"Your blood will run green!" Their chants filled the air.

"The Emerald Blood," Magnus whispered. "We walked into a trap."

13

Fire in the Night

The once peaceful darkness filled with the cries of men and women in the throes of battle. The Emerald Blood marched through portals that ripped through the air around them. Before they knew it, everything had descended into chaos.

On the northern side of the camp, Boram led ten of his squad members into the fight. Magnus looked over and watched Boram turn his body to steel and rush into the enemy lines. He roared with excitement and anger as he clashed with the swordsmen fighting back.

Flaming arrows rained down from the sky, some missing their mark and others burying themselves in the guards gathering themselves for battle. Rhaste went to work, following Neoma's command. She backed into the center of the camp, as far as she could from the enemy front lines, and used her abilities to disrupt their positions and provide whatever cover she could from the arrows streaming through their camp.

Each of their numbers were dropping, but the Emerald Blood brought a far bigger force than they did. They were twice the size reported by the scout. Neoma had already rushed out to her guards, joining the battle without hesitation. She cut her way into the center of one of the enemy lines. They turned their blades on her, swinging violently. She danced around their slashes, landing blow after blow in vital spots. Singlehandedly, a dozen soldiers fell dead at her feet.

"We cannot let them win this night!" she roared. "We are the Royal Guard. We will prevail!"

The clangs of their blades and the cries of the fallen were drowned out by the invigorated response from every guard still standing. Magnus looked down at his hands. Their shaking unnerved him, and he wasn't sure if he would be able to save anyone in his current state. Then a fist slammed against his cheek, knocking him out of his stunned daze.

"You are meant to lead these men. So, get out there and do that!" Rhaste screamed at him.

Magnus stared at her as she rushed back to the battlefield. The metallic taste of the blood in his mouth brought him back to the present. He steadied himself and clenched his fist. His eyes narrowed as he looked at the enemy forces. He focused on the area where they seemed to be firing off abilities more than exchanging blows. There he saw a group of robed members standing around a single person. It was a woman with her face and body cloaked in a black robe. She stood out from the others.

Magnus rushed the line, dodging the flames and earth soaring his way. Their aim was wild, untrained, and it made it harder to predict, but it lacked the precision he was used to and that made it easier to maneuver. Once he was close, he placed three quick blows on the first bandit he could reach, sending them crumpling to the ground. The others surrounded him, using everything they had to take him down.

He whirled around them, getting in close where he had the advantage. His arms felt heavy and his vision began to blur the longer the fight went on. The woman in the black cloak had stopped attacking and watched from behind the others as Magnus tore through them. Her unusual behavior drew his attention for a moment and a blast of fire caught his shoulder. He rolled to the ground, ripping the singed cloth of his cloak.

The burn sent a surge of pain through his arm and his breathing was becoming erratic. He rolled out of the way of the next few blasts that came his way, but his movements were slowing down. The ground shattered in front of him, sending him backward. He howled in pain and grit his teeth. He dug his feet into the ground and pushed himself up, rushing the bandits again. After taking a few more hits, he'd taken them all down. He turned on the witch. She stood still, staring at him from under her hood.

For the first time, he could see her face. She was just a young girl, no more than a teenager. Her jet-black hair and brown eyes were familiar to him, but he was certain he had never met the girl before. What was most concerning was the wave of emotion that emanated from her? It was out of place, but it was strong. It was regret. As though she were far more troubled than one could imagine.

He shook it off. He couldn't afford to care about the feelings of his enemies. Someone as powerful as she was had to be kept close. She had to know more about Cade and his daughter.

"Where is he?" Magnus growled, his chest rose and fell without restraint. "Tell me where Cade is, witch!"

"Why should I tell you that?" She waved her hand in front of her, gesturing to the battlefield. "You've already lost."

Magnus turned and looked out at the camp. Nearly everyone had fallen, lying in pools of blood, their bodies cut up and disfigured by the Emerald Blood. One bandit stood in the middle of the camp. He stood in front of one of the fire pits, holding Rhaste by a handful of her hair. He cackled as he pushed her head towards the flames.

"NO! PLEASE NO!"

Magnus's heart sank to the depths of his stomach. He tried to move towards her, but his body had grown so heavy that he could barely move. As the flames began to touch the side of her face, her screams filled the air with the most guttural and horrifying sound that he had ever heard. Then the bandit suddenly stared into the sky. His face covered in shock and anguish. Rhaste fell to the side, tears pouring from her eyes, writhing in pain. The bandit's body fell to the side and behind him knelt Elias, clutching his side with one hand and his blade in the other.

"Magnus," he called out. "Live!"

He grabbed Rhaste's cloak and they both vanished in a puff of shadows and smoke. Magnus fell to his knees. His stomach churned and he thought any minute that the meat from earlier would find itself on the ground in front of him. Another scream to the side jolted his head upwards. Neoma was still in the heat of battle, one opponent left standing in front of her. Her body was covered in cuts. The rise and fall of her chest was more erratic than his own. He could see that she was on her last legs and the other bandits left standing were advancing on her. Other than himself, she was the last one left standing.

Even Boram, his steel retreating from every inch of his body, was on his knees. They were beaten and he was powerless to help them.

"Do you understand now? The depths of his hatred." The witch spoke up from behind him.

"Why? Why does he hate me? Has he not taken enough from me!"

"The one called Magnus. It is you who took from him. That is what he speaks when he tells me of his hatred. For that, he will ensure you never have anything to care for again."

"I... took from him?" Magnus turned to the witch with disbelief, clambering to his feet. "He murdered my wife. He left me to die on the ground. He took my daughter from me! That's what happened fifteen years ago. I took nothing from him! So, kill me now, or I will tear his lying tongue from his mouth the first chance I get."

"He took your..." the witch muttered.

She stumbled backward; her eyes began to glow white. She gripped the sides of her head and howled in agony. The pain brought her to her knees. Neoma, having slain the last enemy in front of her, rushed towards her while her guard was down. She lunged with her blade. The witch vanished as the sword plunged through the air where her head had been. She reappeared in front of Neoma and placed her hand on the side of Neoma's face, over her eye.

"I will not die here," she whispered.

Her hand burned bright until flames burst from her palm. Neoma's screams dropped Magnus to his knees again. He screamed out for her, but his vision began to fade. He could see almost nothing but the black that was overcoming his sight. Neoma's body fell limp to the ground, the side of her face scorched by the witch's flames.

"That was the last one," the witch said to the other bandits. "Magnus is to be left alive. We're done here."

Magnus crumpled to the ground, fading out of consciousness. The only thing he could make out was the thunderous sound of their footsteps as they marched past him.

"Neo... o... ma." Her name escaped his lips with the last of his energy before he succumbed and fell into darkness.

14

The King's Council

King Mirian's hand crashed down on the top of the wooden table with a *bang*. "That is enough bickering."

The gathered members of the king's council fell silent and stared wide-eyed at their ruler. He was a man who stayed calm in the direst moments, but his patience had run thin. The emergency meeting had been called only a few minutes earlier, dragging most of the councilmen out of bed, but their egregious arguments were more than he could stomach.

"Sire, I do apologize for the way we have acted thus far, but this situation is most daunting indeed. Even you must see that," Councilman Cestian said.

"Of course I know that, Cestian. I sent them out there. I sent my people into a trap and their lives are on my head!" He slammed both hands on the table and his voice seemed to shake the castle walls.

Erelwyn shuffled over to Mirian and leaned in close as he spoke. "My King, now is not the time to lose face in front of your subordinates. You must face this as gracefully as you are able."

"To hell with graceful, Erel. I will not pretend that this has not taken me out of sorts."

"So, it's true then," Talia said from the council room doors. "The servants whisper of a massacre outside our walls. From this meeting, I can only assess that their words bare a terrible truth."

"Talia, you should not be here. I will discuss this with the family another time."

"I am tired of you telling me to walk away, Father. Mideri walks a path far from home. That makes me the eldest heir present. I should be present at these meetings." Talia stomped into the room.

Mirian watched the expression on her face in awe. The flicker of light from the candlelight made her stern gaze hold more than he expected. She looked fiercer than her brother ever had when he stood in the very same room.

"Why don't we all sit and talk this over properly?" suggested Councilman Varros.

"Agreed," Councilman LaMaude responded.

Mirian looked over the members of the king's council and back at his daughter. He let out a deep sigh and nodded, gesturing to the empty chair where Mideri usually sat. Talia puffed her chest out triumphantly and sat in the council seat across from her father. For a moment they sat in silence. They all knew the generalities of the information being presented, but once the report was officially laid out for them, it would all become real.

"Approximately three hours prior to the call of this meeting, our crow returned with word from the scout placed in Grithala," Erelwyn began. "The Emerald Blood knew of our guards' approach. They revealed half of their force and hid the other half. After arriving, the squadrons were ambushed by the full force of the enemy with the help of a witch... there were no survivors."

The heads of the council members hung low over the table. They each imagined the carnage of the battlefield in their own way. King Mirian clenched his fist and grit his teeth to the point of pain in his jaw. He wanted nothing more than to place his sword in Cade's stomach for the bodies he'd piled on top of his previous sins.

"We will send a recovery team to retrieve our people. There's no need for stealth, so send a team that can traverse the mountains as swiftly as possible. We will bring our people back here and give them a proper burial," King Mirian ordered.

Varros passed the report to Cestian after reading it over himself. "Sir, the bodies were disfigured by the witch's flames. I suggest we wrap them in an *elekhat* before they arrive. It would be quite horrifying for their family members to see them in such a state."

"He speaks the truth, sire," LaMaude said. "I shall make the preparations myself."

"Traditional *elekhat* will not be enough," Talia spoke up. "These men and women did not lose their lives in the city as per a normal guard's line of duty. They went beyond our city walls and fought an enemy of the kingdom."

"Then what is it you suggest, my Lady?" asked Cestian.

"I move that we bury them in the ceremonial cloth used

for the Ahndaele. They deserve the same *elekhat* as the warriors who fight on our front lines."

Mirian's heart was heavy with the news received that night, but as he looked up at his daughter, he was filled with pride. The other councilmen looked at her with open mouths, but none could find a reason to disagree with her motion. She was right by all accounts. This was beyond the scope of a normal funeral for a member of the guard. Though none had been promoted, they'd fought the same as any Ahndaele would be expected. Even an Ahndaele rarely met in battle with a witch. In truth, their survival would have been nothing short of a miracle in any of the council's eyes.

"The motion shall be granted," Mirian stated, nodding in Talia's direction. "We shall hold a funeral with a full Valkyrie send-off. For the squadron leaders, Magnus Alexander and Neoma Myrelic, we shall hold a special feast here in the castle. Magnus was like family to myself and my family members. Neoma was family to him. It is only right we host this event."

Cestian whipped his head towards Mirian. "Wait, you sent the Myrelic girl on this mission?"

"Is there an issue with the king's decision, Cestian?" Erelwyn glared in his direction.

"N-no. Her ability was just quite valuable to our kingdom. Losing her is a major blow to our resources is all."

"These are our people, Cestian. *My* people. They are not resources or tools. Losing any one of them is a loss for our people. Losing all of them is a tragedy. Never speak of our people in such a way in this court ever again. Am I understood?" Mirian asked.

"Yes, my Lord. My apologies." Cestian bowed his head.

"Then let us move forward." Mirian stood to address the entire table. "LaMaude, you will gather the *elekhat* for the burials."

"Yes, my Lord. Right away."

"Varros, you are to choose and deploy the recovery team to the specifications I stated earlier. Ensure they are ready to leave at first light and not a minute later."

"I shall have them heading out before the sun can peak the horizon."

"Good. Cestian, you are in charge of handling all logistics for the affair. Make sure the burial plots are ready, food is prepared for the feasts, and the families of the fallen are properly notified when the recovery team returns."

"But m-my King, is that not a job for your—" Cestian stammered.

"You dare question my orders?" Mirian's eyes burned with vibrant blue light.

"N-no, sire. I shall ensure everything is done properly and efficiently."

"As well you should. With this, I hereby call this meeting adjourned. You have your orders. Carry them out at once."

"Sir," they each replied with a low bow before leaving the room.

King Mirian let out a deep sigh and walked back to his throne. He turned slowly and dropped into his seat. He leaned back without restraint, smacking his head into the back of the throne.

"Would Cestian not have been a better option to gather the recovery team? His connections in the Royal Army and

Spy Corps offers him a wider variety of warriors to choose from," Erelwyn asked.

"Perhaps, but I could not excuse his comment from earlier. If he views our people as nothing more than tools, then I shall not allow him to put together the team for such a sensitive mission. Varros is resourceful. He should have no issues. Of that, I can assure you."

"It is rare form for you to lose your temper that way, Father," Talia said. "I know how difficult the loss of Uncle Magnus is, but if you lose yourself whenever those close to us fall, the other council members may doubt your ability to rule."

"Let them doubt me. Let them scream their worries about my ability to rule from the rooftops. If I am to rule from atop a pedestal where my heart need be as cold as the steel of my blade, then I truly would be unfit to lead this kingdom. Remember my daughter, the true measure of a ruler is not his pride. Rather it is what he is willing to sacrifice for the good of his people. Even if that means my throne."

Talia's eyes could not leave her father's. They were sunken and near lifeless. The shadows dancing across his face made it appear hollow. They were alive, yet without heart. He had so much energy before the others left, but now it all seemed to be gone.

"What is it that you would have us do, Father?"

"Simple. The two of you shall do what you asked of me the other night, Talia." Mirian leaned forward. "The two of you shall lead the recovery team. Eliminate any of those Emerald Blood bastards you may encounter."

"Of course, Father. I shall go prepare at once." Talia turned and headed for the door.

Erelwyn bowed and spoke before leaving. "As you wish, my king."

"Erel, one more thing." King Mirian looked up at him, the shadows cast from the candlelight danced across his eyes. "Bring me that scout. Something tells me that he knows more than he's telling us."

Erel nodded and followed Talia out of the room. The court doors slammed shut behind them with a loud *thud*. The sound echoed throughout the now empty court. Mirian let out a deep sigh. He placed his hand on the back of his head and raised an eyebrow at the moisture he felt. When he pulled his hand away, it was covered in blood. He turned and looked at the spot where he'd slammed his head into the chair. Blood trickled down the back of the throne.

"Damn. Teferi will have my head if I bring this back to bed."

15

A Friend from the Past

Magnus took in nothing but darkness around him. Every inch of his body bore the weight of a hundred suits of armor. He kept his eyes shut tight, fearing the image he would bear witness to if he opened them. He wasn't sure how long he'd been out or what had happened since the battle, but he remembered everything that he saw that night. He couldn't bring himself to see it again; their bodies strewn across the battlefield. It was unjust for his guards to be put in such a state.

The smell around him reached his nostrils and his mind was sent into a whirlwind of confusion. He could not smell the metallic scent of blood or the dew on the grass. Even the stench that should linger on his skin was absent. Instead, he smelled eggs and what smelled like fresh meat.

He risked blinking his eyes open and above him was the wooden ceiling of a cabin. He shot up from the table he had been resting on and looked around the unfamiliar oak walls surrounding him. His chest rose and fell with every terrified breath.

"Well if ya wanna go ahead and kill yer'self by rippin' open them stitches I gave ya, be my guest," spoke an unfamiliar voice from behind him.

Magnus looked down at his body and realized he was covered in bandages. The burn on his shoulder felt cool and the places he suffered deeper cuts were stitched and dressed. Everything was still incredibly sore, but she actually had taken care of him.

He looked back at the woman standing over the fire, cooking the food he'd smelled earlier. He could tell by her accent and the way she dressed that she was from No Man's Land. Her long, messy orange hair fell past her waist and the rags she wore for clothing were clearly hand stitched. She looked up to him with a crooked smile that reached up to her eyes.

"I suppose I should thank you. Please, what is your name, so I could thank you properly?"

"You know her name," Neoma's voice floated into the room like a solemn melody.

"Neoma!" Magnus stumbled over to her. "By the ancestors, I thought I'd lost you."

He placed his hand on her face. Bandages covered most of the side of her face; her foretelling eye completely covered. The rest of her body looked much like his own. There was nothing in her expression except despair. He had never seen her in such a state, but he knew what she was feeling and that nothing he said would lift her spirits.

"What do you mean I already know her name? I've never seen her before now," Magnus said.

"True, but I have spoken of her many times. Magnus, meet Yeseni. The only friend I ever made when I was in the orphanage."

"Pleasure to meet ya, Magnus. Like she said, I'm Yeseni, from the Wildlands. No family name to offer. Hence growing up in the orphanage and all."

Yeseni stood up straight and wiped her hands off on the apron wrapped around her waist. She sauntered over to Neoma and placed her lips softly on the injured side of her face. A soft green glow came off her lips where they touched Neoma's face. The tension in Neoma's shoulders seemed to relax a bit before she walked over to the nearest chair and fell into it.

"I see, you're a healer," Magnus said.

"Somethin' of a walkin' pain killer. I'll speed yer healin' up, but it's still mostly natural. I can only turn a couple months into a few days," Yeseni explained.

"I see. Well, thank you again, Yeseni. I don't think either of us would still be alive if weren't for you. We owe you quite the debt."

"Myself more than the others," Neoma added.

"Well, I only had some patchin' up to do. Somebody else gave you a little healin' before I got to ya," Yeseni explained.

"Someone else? I suppose that doesn't matter for now. You mentioned others," Magnus said. "Who else survived?"

"Just Elias and Rhaste."

Memories replayed in front of his eyes. He remembered her screams and Elias's order. His blood ran cold as he looked back at Neoma and her scream rang loud in his ears. Looking at her brought him pain, but he was happy that she was still standing despite the devastating blow she'd been dealt.

"Where are they?" Magnus asked.

"Restin', and you should be doin' the same mister." Yeseni stomped over to him and gently shoved him towards the couch pushed against the wall. "Lay yer ass down before ya open them wounds again."

Elias stepped around the corner moments after his name was mentioned. His torso was wrapped in heavy bandages that showed signs of bleeding through, but he seemed otherwise uninjured.

"I almost thought you disobeyed my orders last night," Elias said. "When we found you yesterday morning, I was certain you were dead. Till you started talking."

"Talking? What did I say?"

Elias glanced over at Neoma then back at Magnus with a smirk. "I don't think you want me to bring that up right now."

"Maybe that's for the best." Magnus cleared his throat while looking over at Neoma who raised her eyebrow at his bashful behavior. "Moreover, I want to thank you for saving Rhaste. You came back at great personal risk."

"Well, the little bird is far more wounded than any of us. Her scars will run deep for many years to come."

"Were her burns that severe?" Neoma asked.

"Her burns were minimal at best, but the damage done to her mind is beyond Yeseni's abilities. What she saw that night — how close she came to death and watching her comrades fall — she's barely able to sleep. I doubt she'd ever be able to face an enemy again."

Silence filled the room. The only sound to be heard was

the crackling of the fire in the hearth. Yeseni wiped her table down and placed out dishes for each of them. She filled their plates and grabbed another before walking to the back of the cabin.

They sat at the table and prepared to dig in, realizing how empty their stomachs felt. Suddenly a crash from the back of the cabin made them jump from the table.

"GET AWAY FROM ME!"

They followed the crash and yelling into the hall. Yeseni stood outside of Rhaste's room, picking up the pieces of a broken plate and spilled food. Her face was full of pain and pity. The playful eyes she showed in the sitting room had been replaced by something empty.

Elias crept past her and tapped lightly on Rhaste's door. "Little bird, it's me. I'm coming in."

"Elias? Elias, please help me," she cried from the other side of the door.

Elias took a deep breath and stepped into the room. Magnus and Neoma helped Yeseni finish cleaning up the mess. Once they finished, they stood in front of the door. Neoma gasped at the scene in front of her. Rhaste was curled into a ball in Elias's arms with tears streaming endlessly from her eyes. Her hair was singed on one side with light burns scarring her face. Her body was covered in bruises and fresh cuts. A dagger lay on the floor on the other side of the room still stained with what they could only assume was her blood.

"Let it out, little bird. I'm here for you." Elias stroked her head and Magnus wasn't sure, but for a moment, he thought he saw a tear form in his eye.

They closed the door quietly and stepped back into the sitting room. Yeseni sat on the couch with her head in her hands. Her soft sobs could be heard the closer they got.

"Yeseni, this wasn't your fault," Neoma tried to comfort her.

"It's ain't that. Just seeing her like that. Reminded me of my sis. Before I went to the orphanage, she and I were always together. She went off deeper in the Wildlands one day, gave me that stuffed toy I gave ya before she left. She was hopin' to find a tribe for us to join, didn't want me to be in danger. When she came back, she won't the same no more. A lot like that girl in there. Took her six months before she took her own life. I'm just worried about yer friend. Hit a little close to home I suppose."

"Wait, if that stuffed toy was all you had left of your sister, why'd you give it to me?"

"'Cause you looked so much like her back then. When I saw ya, I felt like it was me getting a second chance to give it back to the sister I knew. Thought maybe somehow, I'd have her back then. Even a little."

Neoma wrapped her arms around Yeseni. Magnus walked over to the coat rack in the corner and grabbed his cloak. He tossed it over his shoulders and started towards the door.

"Where the hell do you think you're going?" Elias asked from the hallway.

"I'm going to find that scout. There's no way a force that big could have hid without someone with their ear to the ground in Grithala hearing about it. He knew more than he told us and look what happened. So, I'm going to find out what he knows."

Elias stomped his foot on the ground in front of Magnus.

Tendrils formed from the shadows around them, shot up from the ground, and wrapped themselves around him. Magnus grunted and struggled against the tendrils, but they had him gripped tight.

"You have the most injuries out of all of us. You'll be going nowhere. Whether we find out what he knows or not, we can do nothing if you aren't properly healed."

"Let me go, Elias. I've dragged the lot of you into my mess more than enough at this point."

"Elias is right," Neoma said, "if anyone is going to go, it's me."

"Neoma—" Elias started.

"You need to be here. You're the only one who has the power to keep him from running off and doing something stupid. Besides, if Rhaste needs you, I want you to be here. At least for now."

Elias nodded to her and released Magnus from the tendrils. "We're a day and a half away from Grithala here. You have four days to be back here before I let the dog loose and we come looking for you."

"Understood."

Magnus stepped forward and placed his hand on her shoulder. "Neoma are you certain? Without the use of your eye, you could be in more danger than usual."

"Was it not you that told me I was more than just my eye? I will be fine, Magnus. I'll bring the scout back here and Elias can question him. We'll get our answers."

Magnus nodded and stepped back. Neoma grabbed her cloak and turned back towards them after she opened the door.

"Take care of them, Yeseni. I'll be back soon."

"Come back to me," Magnus whispered.

"I will."

16

Traitors & Depravity

Whispers and rumors spread quickly around Grithala. The loud battle from the other night caught the attention of every person in the town. Some thought that the kingdoms were in all-out war again and started stockpiling supplies. Others spoke of the return of the Fade and brave heroes protecting the town. Every rumor in the town reached Cade's ear and the more ridiculous the rumor, the louder he laughed at their petty gossip.

Their temporary housing in Grithala's council building was filled with the Emerald Blood members that had survived the night in question. The last few days had been filled with wine, ale, and the finest food the townspeople could bring them. Town natives served the Emerald Blood members as the bandits celebrated their victory. Uyala sat at the front of the room atop Cade's lap. She, along with many other men and women from Grithala, had been stripped bare for the bandits' amusement.

"I'm proud of all of you," Cade yelled out to them. "You all did exactly what we needed to return home victorious."

The bandits roared with excitement. They raised their drinks in the air and downed whatever they had left. Some pulled the men and women serving them to the side and abused them for their own pleasure. Others struck each other like animals testing their strength. Cade looked out at the sea of chaos in front of him, smiling from ear to ear.

The door to the council building creaked open. The party was in full swing and no one except Cade noticed the scout creep into the room. He pushed his way through the sea of ravenous bodies and fell to his knees in front of Cade.

"It's good to see that everyone who returned seems to be in good spirits, sir," he said.

"Yes, you did well boy. Magnus and his weaklings clearly knew nothing of our plans."

"Of course. I would never betray you. I am loyal to the Emerald Blood."

"Oh? Loyalty is a funny word isn't it." Cade smiled maliciously down at the scout. "We always boast about those loyal to us, but what does it really mean? That they follow your orders when you ask them to? That they'll die for you?"

"Of course, sir. I would do whatever you asked." The scout looked up at him with sweat pouring down his forehead.

"Anything?"

"Yes. Anything, sir."

"Then gut yourself with your own blade," Cade ordered.

The scout looked up at Cade with horror in his eyes. "B-but I thought I did everything you asked, sir. I thought I did well."

"You did. That's why I'm allowing you to make your death swift. You've outlasted your use to me, and I don't make a habit of keeping useless toys lying about the floor."

"I don't understand. I'm still loyal to you. I always have been."

"Always? Were you not once *loyal* to Astoria? Your loyalties have changed since then. That's the problem with loyalty. The only people who are truly loyal are those who are already dead."

"Please, sir. Don't make me do this," the scout pleaded.

"Do you think you could still serve some use to me?" Cade asked.

"I can. I'm sure of it."

"Very well then." Cade leaned over to Uyala and whispered something in her ear.

She smiled at his words and ran her hands over his body and into his vest. When she was done, she slid off his lap and walked over to the scout. She pushed him over with one hand and mounted him, moving her hips sensually over him. Then she pulled her hand from behind her back and plunged a knife into his chest with a wicked smile painted on her face.

He gasped as the blade slid deeper into his body. He coughed and sputtered, covering Uyala in blood. Uyala lifted the blade and stabbed down again and again. She kept going, without a word; only a smile spread across her lips.

When the scout's body fell limp and lifeless, she pulled the dagger out once more and pushed herself up from the ground. Uyala sauntered over to Cade, smile still spread wide, and dropped into his lap. She sank into him, pleased that she had done what he asked. He stroked her cheek, but his eyes stayed on the butchered corpse that lay at his feet.

"I never understood your amusement at such vulgarities," a familiar voice spoke beside him.

Cade turned his head, and his smile grew at the sight of Erelwyn. "Pain and death are a form of art if the watcher can appreciate it for its beauty."

"Detestable." Erelwyn clicked his tongue. "Nevertheless, you held up your end of the bargain. We've just confirmed the casualties on the battlefield, difficult as it was considering the charred faces and bodies."

Cade's amused smile turned sinister. He didn't want Erelwyn learning that he let Magnus live. The extra bodies added to the charred corpses were his own dead bandits, dressed to fit the part. As far as anyone knew, no survivors walked away.

"However, next time," Erelwyn continued, "put a leash on that witch. No recognizable faces means that there will be questions whether the people there are who they say they are. We're also short one body. Are you certain you got them all?"

Cade raised an eyebrow and stood from his chair. He was sure they had placed enough bodies for the three that got away; Magnus and that irritating Shadow who saved the girl. He figured Erelwyn must be bluffing, to ensure that his trust was not misplaced.

"I'm certain, dog. Now run back to your master and tell him what you've learned. If anyone with you were to find out that you were seen here speaking with me, I imagine he would not be so pleased."

"Believe me, I'd rather not stand is this house of debauchery for any longer. Though I was meant to bring the scout back as well. It seems you've saved me the trouble of killing him myself. I'll be off with his body then."

"And what will you tell your master?"

"Simply another crime you'll have to take credit for. I'm sure you're terrified of what he'll do when he hears the news."

"I'm shaking in my boots." Cade's laugh shook Erelwyn to his core.

Erelwyn shook his head and stepped over to the scout's body. He placed his hand on his mangled torso and they both disappeared in a puff of smoke. Cade turned back to Uyala who wore a confused expression on her face as she watched the situation unfold. He pushed past her and stood in front of his bandit guild members, taking a moment to absorb it all.

"Brothers and sisters, the time has come for us to return home. Enjoy this night, for tomorrow we return to Reissgard!"

"My village is on the way." Uyala looked up at him with a hopeful glint in her eye. "Can we retrieve my son on the way there?"

Cade stroked her cheek. "Of course. As I told you. He will be free to do as he chooses. Once we return home, I will send him on his journey to the Wildlands. It will be one he never forgets."

17

Little Bird

Magnus paced about the cabin. Every noise from the other side of the door prompted him to burst through it and check the surrounding area. For three days, he did nothing but pace. Yeseni was certain he was pressing a permanent pattern of his footsteps into her floor. Elias spent most of his time getting Rhaste to move further out of the bedroom.

Her nightmares had not stopped, but she was beginning to see reality a bit more for what it was, instead of seeing the faces of the Emerald Blood everywhere she looked. By the third day, she had made it to the sitting room, but she could only sit there when the hearth was empty. The crackle of the fire sent her into an episode similar to the day she had attacked Yeseni. None of them blamed her, they could see no reason to. They wanted to help her, but that seemed more difficult than they would have thought.

In truth, they wondered if the night had been worse on her than them because she had something to lose. Her fear of death, the trauma she endured, was more painful than the scars they bared. The rest of them, had they died on that bat-tlefield, would have lived lives that they believed served their purpose. She had far more to give. They were all cut deep, but she showed more strength even in her state, because day by day, she showed them that she still wanted to move forward.

Today was no different. The hearth was still and the four of them occupied the sitting room in relative silence. The only sound was Magnus's repetitive footsteps across the wooden floors. Night had fallen on the fourth day. By morning, the two of them would set out to retrieve Neoma. Magnus was unsuited to patience. His eyes darted between the door and his cloak every few seconds.

"Why do we not set out?" he asked Elias. "Night has fallen. The day is done and she has not returned."

"We wait until morning, Magnus. Trust her. She will re-turn."

"You should not worry so much, sir," Rhaste whispered. "She is mighty. If she returns with blood on her clothes, I doubt it will be hers."

Magnus knew they were right, but his own worries plagued him. Only he was meant to survive that night. If the others were hunted due to this grudge Cade held, it would be on his head. Convinced by his own thoughts, he rushed over to grab his cloak and reached out for the door. Before his hand could press against the wood, it swung open. Neoma stood in the doorway, panting, her hands placed on her knees.

"Neoma, you've returned. Are you alright?" Magnus asked.

"I am fine. I met no opposition on my journey."

"Where is the scout? Did something happen?" Elias asked.

Neoma straightened herself up and moved into the sitting

room. Magnus closed the door behind her and followed. They all sat down and Neoma took a deep breath before recounting what she'd seen.

"I made it to the town just in time. The Emerald Blood was still there. They had taken over the council building and were celebrating their evils."

"When you say the Emerald Blood was there...?" Magnus asked.

"Yes," Neoma looked at him with shadows over her eyes, "I saw Cade."

Magnus clenched his fist. Once again, he felt like bursting through that door and racing to Grithala, but even he was smart enough to see that he would surely lose his life if he fought in his current state.

"What did you learn?" Elias asked.

"The scout was indeed working with Cade. I slipped into the council building shortly after he did, and I heard as much of their conversation as I could. The scout was meant to give us only some information so that their ambush wouldn't trace back to him, but it didn't matter. Soon after he spoke with Cade, a woman companion of Cade's killed him." As the images of the woman sitting over the scout's body replayed in her mind, all the color drained from Neoma's face.

"I've never seen something so haunting," she continued. "She took so much pleasure from driving that knife into his chest again and again. After he was dead, she just climbed into Cade's lap like she was his loyal servant. Smiling as though she hadn't just mutilated a man."

A low growl escaped Elias's throat. "They say Cade has the power to influence people's state of mind. He's not known to fraternize with members of his clan. Most likely that woman was a local that he manipulated into doing his dirty work for him. Even if she were to become sound of mind again, he'll have control over her just for what she's now done."

"Just how many lives will he ruin before something more is done about this? Shouldn't we tell the king? If we know where he is, and it's in Astorian territory, he can send the Royal Army in this time," Rhaste said.

"That's the issue." Neoma swallowed the lump in her throat and looked between Elias and Magnus. "The king's right hand, the one known as Erelwyn, was also in the council building that night."

"Neoma, are you certain that it was him? Are you certain Erelwyn was with the Emerald Blood?" Magnus asked.

"I saw him, heard him, heard his name, and I heard him speak of the king. As far as I can tell, the king knows nothing of Erelwyn's betrayal, but even if we were able to tell him now, it would be for nothing. The Emerald Blood won't be in Grithala anymore."

"They've made plans to move? Did you happen to find out where?" Elias asked.

"That's the biggest issue of them all. If we wanted another shot at Cade, it could mean all-out war. The Emerald Blood is a Reissgardian guild now. They've already made plans to return."

"So, to get to him we have to breach another kingdom's territory. If we return home first and inform the king, he will never allow us to march into their territory. If we go without informing him, as citizens of Astoria the blame for our actions would fall on the kingdom and all-out war could ensue. Our forces are not prepared for a war with Reissgard. We would ultimately risk losing far more than they do." Elias spoke out loud, but his words seemed directed at no one in particular.

They sat in silence and continued to try and organize their thoughts. The options left to them were not kind, but they were sure that they all hoped for the same end goal. Cade had to die. As long as he remained, the Emerald Blood would be a plague on the land they called home. His very existence was a stain on Aévan's history.

Magnus's head shot up and he grabbed everyone's attention. "Erelwyn would never be able to leave the city walls without the king's order. He was likely sent there with the recovery team to retrieve our fallen comrades, but if my memory serves, only I was meant to walk away that night. Cade would not be so happy if his efforts had failed."

"I did hear Erelwyn say something about a body missing. Though I couldn't make out the entire conversation. If he believes us all to be dead, then that is likely what he will tell the king," Neoma added.

"If Erelwyn believes one person escaped, then perhaps that is what we should give him." Rhaste's eyes were locked on the ground, but every else's fell on her.

"What're you going on about?" Yeseni asked.

"Perhaps it's time that I return home. Or rather, I let the recovery team find me."

"Little bird, have you gone mad? Who's to say that there are not others on the recovery team under Cade or Erelwyn's thumb? You could walk right into another trap. We won't be able to go with you." Elias leaned forward and drew her gaze. His eyes were fierce, narrowed to assert his concerns. He often gave his opinions without restraint, but this time, Magnus could tell that he was struggling to say everything he wanted. There was malice streaming from him that he had never sensed before. It wasn't directed, not at anyone in the room. It was more like it was surrounding Rhaste. As though he would use his hatred to protect her from anything else that might harm her.

"Elias, I thank you for everything you have done. I, and all the others, were wrong about you from the start, but I must do this. I am still a warrior. Whether I can fight or not, that will never change. How can I expect to leave my family alone in a kingdom being manipulated by a traitor like Erelwyn and live a normal life?"

"But—"

"If the members of the recovery team are still loyal to Astoria, then I will receive safe passage home. Erelwyn doesn't know that I am aware of his betrayal. I can receive an audience with the king to discuss the events that happened on our journey. There I will reveal the truth. The entire court will be present. He can hide no longer."

"Yes, but that is only betting that the members of the recovery team are indeed loyal to the kingdom."

"That's a risk that I must take. You all have your own path that you must take." She wrapped her arms around Elias. "This is mine." She stood up from the couch and took a deep breath. "I'll gather my things."

She walked to the back and put together a small pack. She sighed as she walked back out into the sitting room. Everyone stood around her. They looked at her with fear, pride, and some with deep sorrow.

"Are you sure about this, Rhaste?" Neoma asked.

"If the recovery team was in Grithala a day and a half ago, then they should be passing by here soon. They likely set out the following morning. I'll place myself in their path and should be discovered by midday. This is the only way to return without suspicion. I would never make it back on my own."

"You be careful out there, guard. Remember, you're one of us. We always see the mission through," Magnus said.

"Always," she responded.

"Oh, come here you." Yeseni tossed her arms around Rhaste and pulled her in close. "I know we ain't got on the whole time you was here, but I want you to be safe."

"Thank you. For everything you've done. I know I was difficult, but you continued to show me kindness. I will never forget that."

Elias grabbed Rhaste's arm and lead her through the doorway. They stood outside of the door and he stared at her, like a father waiting to release his daughter out into the world for the first time.

"Little bird, it seems that clipped wing of yours is healed. I hate to say it, but perhaps you are ready to fly again. Perhaps it's just me who isn't ready to see you go," he whispered.

"Why do you care for me so? You look at me as though I was precious to you. You call me little bird, as though you've known me your entire life."

"You reminded me of someone when I first saw you. At first, I paid it no mind, but then when you fell from that cliff, it was like I was losing her all over again. I couldn't let that happen. Though, I must remember that you are not her. You are much older, much stronger than she was able to grow to be." The corner of his lip turned up for a moment, then fell as the sad memories came to the forefront of his mind.

"Well, regardless. We are family now. I will return home. Promise me, when you are able, you will write to me. Let me know that you're okay. All of you."

"I will," he said.

"Could you call me that name again? Just one more time?" she asked.

"Fly safe." He kissed her forehead and smiled. "Little bird."

She smiled, a tear slowly drifting down her cheek. She turned back to the others, saluting Magnus and Neoma, waving at Yeseni, then turned her back to them and walked off into the moonlit night.

Magnus and Neoma stepped out of the cabin and joined Elias as he watched her back. Soon she was out of sight and only they were left standing beneath the night sky.

Elias spoke first, still looking at the spot where Rhaste had disappeared "She's right. We have our own path to choose."

"I cannot ask you two to follow where I must go. Your lives have been entangled in my mess far too much already," Magnus said.

"I thought you'd say something like that. You're going to Reissgard. I would expect nothing else. How will you avoid starting a war?" Neoma asked.

Magnus pulled his cloak from around his shoulders. He ran his hands over the Astorian Royal Guard insignia sewn into the fabric. He thought about everything that insignia gave him; everything he'd earned along the way. He wrapped his hand around it and tore the fabric, ripping the insignia from it and tossing it to the side.

"Even if I am Astorian no more, I will ensure the people's safety. To do that, I have died, and I must remain dead. So, I won't go there as a member of the guard. I will go as me and me alone."

"I always thought you were such a fool." Elias chuckled and let out a deep sigh. "It seems I was right."

"How do you figure?"

"Because you don't get it. Not one bit. You're not going anywhere alone. You're not the only one who is dead. I never existed in the first place. So, where you go, I go."

"Elias."

Neoma tossed her own cloak over her shoulders. Magnus looked down and saw that her insignia was also gone. The fabric had already begun to set after it was torn.

"Neoma, you—"

"The moment I heard him say he was going to Reissgard, I knew the decision you would make. I knew the decision I would make. I took it off my cloak before I made it back. Elias is right. You're not alone. Not anymore. None of us are."

"I see. You're both bigger fools than I am. Well, if that's the decision you've made, then we have a long journey ahead of us. This won't end until we finally take him down. In truth, I'm happy that you're both with me."

"Well, that's all well and good, but it ain't as though yer all makin' a quick trip," Yeseni spoke up from behind them, her hands on her hips. "It's a week to Reissgard from here, and that's if ya only stop for about two hours a day. So, get your asses in here, lemme speed yer healing up a bit more."

"Yeseni, that'll drain you far too much. We can't ask that of you," Neoma said.

"Yer forgettin' I'm from the Wildlands. Cade's been a bastard before he came here, and he always will be. I want that bastard dead too. If I gotta sleep for a couple days 'cause I used a bit too much power, that's a price I'm willing to pay."

"Alright then," Magnus spoke up, "then let's say it here and now. This is Cade's final week. Tomorrow, we begin his end."

18

Alchemy

The journey to Reissgard was peaceful. At least, that's how it appeared on the outside. In truth, the length of their journey was daunting. Every step closer added weight on their shoulders until the pressure of the world bore down on them. They moved quickly, not wanting to let up their pace except to recover for a couple of hours at night. At that time, they ate quickly and slept even faster. Each night, one person slept for the entire first hour while the other two ate first. One of the two would then sleep and one kept guard. The first one asleep would be woken after the first hour so the last one could sleep. Every night they rotated who would get the near two hours of sleep so they could retain some semblance of full energy before pressing on again.

They did their best to avoid any contact with others while they made their way to Reissgard. They passed merchant caravans and small towns and villages, but only stopped once to refill their water and supplies and set out again. Before the week was up, they found themselves at the base of the mountains where Reissgard stood.

The view from the bottom of the mountain was breathtaking. Had it not been for the nature of their journey, they might have taken time to admire the landscape. The black stone that made up the majority of the mountain range was intricately carved out to form the stairway up into the city's borders. The bridge at the top spanned miles across a volcanic lake. The bridge was filled with passersby, from merchants and everyday citizens to travelers, explorers, and refugees.

"How do you suggest we get into the city?" Elias asked. "I could pop us in, but I can only take one at a time. Someone would definitely notice if I came back for the other."

"Shelf your worries, friend. Let me handle this one," Magnus replied.

They joined the line of refugees looking for safe haven in the city. Some came to escape the dangerous creatures and tribes of No Man's Land, and others feared for their lives in the smaller townships that were in bandit territories. Astoria had their own refugees hoping to gain citizenship daily, but Reissgard was much closer to many of the smaller towns and villages, so they received far more refugees than Astoria. This gave them the perfect opportunity to blend into the crowd with their hoods raised.

As they approached the front of the line, they could hear the questions the guards asked each person attempting to gain access.

"Name?" The first guard, a stocky man with a long scar down the side of his face, spoke to a man dressed in rags with his arms around his children.

"Velerus, sir. Velerus Hawkswain," the man answered.

The guard continued without looking up from his parchment. "Reason for sanctuary?"

"The bandits in Thorrel village have taken everything from us. They say if I show my face again, they'll take my children." Magnus could feel the fear emanating from him and it filled him with sorrow.

"Children's names?"

"Valtir and Trimela."

"Skills or services you can provide?" the guard asked.

"I was a farmer, sir. That is all I know how to do."

"Entry denied. Please move from the line," the guard ordered.

Velerus fell to his knees, begging the guard to reconsider. Another guard, a hulking man with a thick beard, stepped forward and kicked him to the side. Velerus clutched his stomach and writhed in pain on the ground. The guards laughed and shoved his children to the side before moving on to the next person in line.

"Since when has Reissgard's immigration been so wicked?" Elias sneered in the guard's direction.

"Something is different. Perhaps the council has made some changes." Magnus said.

Velerus gathered himself and his children and started back across the bridge. Magnus reached out to him, grabbing his arm, and pulling him to the side without drawing too much attention to himself.

"Please, sir. I have nothing." Velerus trembled at Magnus's grip and looked up at him wide-eyed.

"Quiet," Magnus whispered, "take this coin and head to

Astoria. Ask for a guard named Rhaste and tell her that a friend of hers sent you from Reissgard. She will help you. Now go."

Velerus grabbed the small silver coin that Magnus handed him and tears began to stream down his face. He opened his mouth to thank him, but Magnus jerked his head to the side, signaling Velerus to leave at once. Velerus nodded and grabbed his kids, heading down the bridge with renewed confidence in their situation.

"How are you certain he will make it all that way? He has no means of surviving the journey," Elias said.

"He will make it," Magnus replied. "He will make it because he cannot afford to die."

Elias was baffled by the confidence with which he delivered such a prediction, but he had far more faith in Magnus now than he did before their journey began. The guards let the next two men enter without any trouble — one was a miner, the other a blacksmith, skills useful in a mountain city. They were next. Before the guard had time to ask their names, Magnus began to hum a tune. The tune itself was discordant, but as long as they heard it, his plan would work. The guards looked up at them and blinked their eyes a few times, before stepping aside and letting them enter the city.

"It seems your abilities are useful for something other than telling stories," Neoma joked.

Magnus smiled and walked through the city gates with Neoma and Elias in tow.

The lowest level of the city was a dilapidated ghetto compared to the levels above. Small dwellings made of wooden posts and cloth filled the streets. Some of the shops, carved from the stone of the mountain, held wares that were crudely made or food that looked to be near rotting.

As though the look of the level itself wasn't sad enough, the people walking about the streets were no more joyful to watch. Many of their faces were sunken in and painted with dark circles as though they had not eaten or slept for days.

"What has become of this city? The people of Reissgard have always been prosperous. Have the guilds forsaken them?" Elias asked.

"Is this not how things usually are?" Neoma looked around and took in the horrible circumstances surrounding them.

"You've never left the city, so you wouldn't know. What you would know is that the guilds of Reissgard run the city, but they normally ensure every level and every citizen is taken care of. That is why life in Reissgard is sought after by many refugees. This... this is not normal."

They walked through the streets and watched as children played, the only ones with any life about them; the older men and women shambled past them. They shook their heads and ducked into a nearby tavern to figure out what their next plans were. Their arrival turned heads, but none seemed too interested in their presence. Only one person's eyes followed them. A woman sitting at the bar. Her bright red hair made her stand out amongst the crowd. She met Elias's gaze and instead of looking away as though she were not staring, she smiled and waved at him like they were lifelong friends.

Elias was suspicious, but he was sure he knew no one in Reissgard, so he ignored her for now, but he made sure to keep an eye on her movements while they remained in the bar. The three of them moved to the back of the room and sat in a booth as far from any others as they could. The barmaid crept over, looking as broken as the others.

"What can I get for you?" her voice was raspy and dry.

"Three ales, please," Neoma replied.

The barmaid nodded and walked off to the kitchen without another word.

"As much as the state of this level disturbs me. We need to focus on the matter at hand. Somehow, we have to figure out where Cade is and how to get to him without taking on the entire Emerald Blood," Elias whispered.

"I know where he is," the woman from the bar said, standing at the end of their table.

They all jumped and looked over at the amused smile on her face. This was the first time any of them got a good look at her. The bright red hair contrasted heavily with her milky white skin. She wore leather armor and a red cloak that was duller than her hair. Two small daggers were sheathed in leather and strapped to her thighs. Despite her bright colors, her aura was much more intimidating. She stood with the presence of someone who was willing to take on all three of them without hesitation.

"Well, you just gonna stare at me?" She leaned down and peered at their confused expressions.

"What business do you have with us?" Neoma asked.

"You're looking for Cade and his criminal guild, and my guild has been waiting for you, so I figure it's a win-win if I came over and introduced myself."

"What do you mean your guild is looking for us? Who are you?" Magnus asked.

"Follow me. This isn't my story to tell." She turned around

and spoke again before starting to the door. "If you're hesitant on trusting me, just know, you're in foreign territory and that little trick you pulled on the guards isn't going to work on me."

They looked at each other and decided that they were too short on options not to go. They kept their eyes on their surroundings as they followed her out of the tavern and up the first flight of steps to the second level of the city.

The second level was in a better state than the first, but not by much. The people still looked as though they were starving and struggling, but there were fewer makeshift homes and the shops had better stock. Most of Reissgard was carved directly out of the inside of the mountain, so the lower levels could be seen if you looked below and the upper levels were harder to see without climbing the stairs.

Looking behind him, Magnus could tell that things were darker beneath them than their small glimpse had shown them. "What happened here?"

"What do you mean?" the woman asked.

"The people in the city. They look as though everything has been taken from them. Has the council given up on them?"

"You're right. Everything was taken from them. It's not as simple as the council choosing to abandon the lower levels. They were forced to."

"Forced?" Elias asked.

"Give you three guesses as to who did it."

"He has that much influence over them? How is that possible?" Magnus sped up to walk beside her as he spoke.

"Easy, he's on it." She bounded up the steps and into the

third level of the city, sauntering past the guards as they looked at her guild crest.

"It seems your guild is of some prominence here as well considering not a single guard has attempted to slow our ascent," Elias said.

"Our leader was once a member of the council as well. It was Cade who took his seat when the Emerald Blood first came to Reissgard fifteen years ago, though they were operating under a different name at the time. Since no one would allow such a criminal guild to enter the city so easily."

"He gave the falsehoods up once he gained a seat, didn't he?" Magnus clenched his fist as they continued on. "Cade's far too proud to sit atop a throne like that and not wave his flag."

"Correct. Once he was on the council, it was too late. Rules were honored and he kept his seat. That's when the changes began. The weak were pushed further and further down in the city. Cade strongarmed the council into only providing for those who were of *use* to the city. Everyone else got scraps. Crime went up, lives were ruined, and people started to die."

"Why does no one do anything about it?" Neoma asked.

"Our guild was the strongest the city had to offer. Our leader sat at the top of the council as a man of kindness and virtue for many years. However, even we can't beat a witch. As long as she is with them, everyone is too terrified to go up against the Emerald Blood. Then, we got word of you and your band of merry men taking him on outside of Grithala. We thought you were insane until we discovered that you actually made it out alive and you were headed this way."

"How could you have possibly known that?" Magnus asked.

"You pass many people on a long journey. You often forget many of their faces, but not all of them forget yours. One of our members was a survivor from the tragedy in Crowind. Something I'm sure you are quite familiar with. She remembered you. Said you were the reason her family was able to escape because you stood up to Cade. Then you did it again outside of Grithala when she was on reconnaissance. Then she saw you headed this way. Made it here the day before you. You've likely seen her many times, but like I said, you forget faces that mean nothing to you when you're on a long journey. That's what your life has been Magnus Alexander, one long ass journey."

"You know quite a lot about me I see. Yet you have yet to tell us something as simple as your name."

"It's Ember, isn't it?" Elias asked.

Magnus and Neoma looked at him with raised brows. Not only were they unsure how he knew her name, but he said it with anger. Magnus could feel the hatred rising once more from him.

"I was wondering how long it would take you to put that together." She walked forward and stopped in front of a large guildhall with red paint accentuating the black stone the building was carved from.

She turned and faced them, gesturing towards the building. "This is my guild hall. We're Reissgard's number two guild, Alchemy."

Elias lunged forward, his face contorted with anger. He held his hand out, manifested his *Sygerth* and stabbed at her.

She unsheathed her dagger and blocked his strike with ease. Her hands moved so fast that Magnus could barely see her movements.

"Elias, what is the meaning of this?" Magnus asked.

"Remember the story I told you? The one about my father being murdered?" Elias pointed his dagger at Ember.

"You think you know everything don't you?" Ember smirked and twirled her dagger between her fingers.

"I know you killed my father! I saw the report. Your name burned into the ground where his camp was. Nothing but his hand with his wedding ring on it found at the scene. They tracked you back here then told us there was nothing more they could do. I almost forgot about it, but as you talked, I started putting it all together. You took him from us."

"Quiet down, boy." A gruff voice from behind Ember drew their attention away from their fighting.

An older man with long white hair and a scraggly gray beard walked out of the guild hall wearing his own red cloak. This one was more ornate than Ember's. His arms were set across his chest, hands in his sleeves as he walked forward. When he stood in front of Elias, he pulled his hands from his sleeve and they noticed that his left hand was missing. Where it should have been was a bandaged stump. He reached out and placed his hand on Elias's cheek and smiled.

"It has been far too long. Welcome to my guild, son."

19

The Witch

"One! Two!"

Every punch sent a cloud of dust into the air. Cade's heavy blows against the sack of rice caused it to burst at the seams. He stared at the floor while the rice spilled out of the bag like a granular waterfall. His eyes stayed lock on them until the last grain fell atop the pile and the room fell silent.

He couldn't get his mind off of Erelwyn's question that night in Grithala. *What does he mean one body short?* The words played endlessly in his mind. He was certain they could not have messed things up. He wanted everything to move flawlessly. He needed them to. Tomorrow he would be married, and he would finally take what was left of Magnus's pitiful little life. He refused to forgive him, for uprooting everything he had all those years ago.

Cade screamed out in frustration and pulled at the rice bag on the hook in front of him. The bag tore off, but so did the hook and the section of the stone ceiling it was attached to. He crushed the bag in his hand. His chest rose and fell quickly with each hulking breath as he imagined ripping Magnus apart again and again.

Then he saw images of the past. Visions of her. He thought back to the time they spent in the Wildlands and who he was becoming because of her. She was the only person who ever stood above him. He roared in frustration again as the images began to fade from the forefront of his mind.

"Sir," a member of the Emerald Blood said behind him.

Cade whipped around with his face still contorted in anger. "What!"

"Th-there's news to report, sir. Gemeline is calling for you in the war room." The bandit backed out of the door.

Cade tossed the bag to the ground and walked towards the hallway. The bandit was already gone, his footsteps echoing up the stairs. Cade stomped up every step and beat open every door in his path. He had no patience for obstacles today. Everything was getting under his skin because of Erelwyn's simple question.

He barged into the war room with little grace. The small number of lieutenants gathered jumped to their feet and saluted him as he made his way to his seat at the head of the table.

"Sit. I don't care to wait for this news. Let me hear it," he barked.

"Yes, sir. In truth, I'm not sure if this news would be received as good or bad. I'm only certain you would want to know," Gemeline said.

"Hurry, Gemeline. My patience is growing thinner with each word."

"Right, sir. One of our scouts was skulking around the Barrows this morning and he caught sight of three refugees. He said that he followed them because one of them fit the description you gave for our target in Grithala. Upon a closer examination, he was able to confirm it was indeed Magnus Alexander. Apparently, he has made his way into Reissgard."

Cade leaned forward, his anger turning into sinister excitement. "Did he track his movements?"

"Yes, sir. That's where the information becomes a bit more concerning. Magnus was not alone. Apparently, he was traveling with two companions. A woman and a man that fit the description of the assassin that vanished from the battlefield."

"So, he brought the spy and the girl he escaped with. I was aware those two lived, though I'm surprised they would come along with him. What else have they been up to?"

"It seems, sir..." Gemeline swallowed hard. "They have come into contact with Ember of the Alchemy Guild. She brought them to the guildhall yesterday afternoon. That's all we know for now."

The lieutenants held their breath as they watched Cade. The information was sparse, and they were unsure how he would react to so little intel on someone he had made them aware of. However, it wasn't his anger that made their blood run cold. Instead, he sat back in his chair with a wide smile that made him resemble a wolf baring its fangs. His eyes were glazed with the bloodthirsty hunger he felt in the pit of his stomach.

"He's here. I've been waiting fifteen years to take everything from you. I was going to let you live. I was going to let you suffer through a hellish eternity of your own pitiful loneliness. It seems your ancestors call to you sooner than I thought. If he is so willing to walk into the jaws of the beast, then I'll rip his throat out with my own teeth."

"W-what should we do, sir?" another lieutenant asked.

"Do? There's nothing for you to do. Nothing has changed. Tomorrow we will continue as planned. The ceremony will be much more interesting than I could have imagined."

"But, what of Alchemy? Are you not concerned about Elijah attempting to take his seat back on the council?"

Cade's smile turned to a grimace. "Oh? *Should I* be concerned?"

"I-I—"

"Are you telling me that you believe that old fool could challenge me to a duel and win?" Cade rose from his seat and walked over to where the terrified lieutenant sat. "I would think that *you* would sooner have a chance of winning against me than he would. So, Lieutenant, would you like to test your doubts? Would you like to face off with me and see if I stand to lose to Elijah?"

The lieutenant leaned as far back as his chair would allow. His entire body shook. Sweat pooled around him as Cade's face inched closer.

"N-no, sir. I don't wish to fight you," he replied.

"That's what I expected. Get out of my sight." The lieutenant jumped from his seat and barreled to the door. "All of you! Leave me!"

Gemeline and the rest of the lieutenants gave him one final salute and marched out of the war room. Cade paced around the table, staring at the map of Reissgard in the center. He looked at the Heights with his eyes narrowed on the spot where the Alchemy Guild's hall sat. His body trembled and his breathing hastened.

"I can feel you getting closer, Magnus. Can you feel me? Can you sense death, standing on your doorstep?" he whispered.

"Your obsession will be the end of you. You continue on like this and the fruits of your labor will not come to bear," the witch spoke from the doorway.

"My love, what are you doing here? I thought you and the others were going to celebrate tonight?"

"Do not give me your false love. You and I both know I only agreed to this marriage to solidify the Emerald Blood's power. Your power is my own. Nothing more."

"You seem much colder than usual. You don't believe my love is real. Why?" Cade asked.

The witch paced around to the opposite end of the table, her eyes locked on the map. "I have seen what your love gives those who you deem worthy enough to receive it. It is nothing but pain and anguish. You shower me with affection, but I know it to be untrue. I've seen other girls my age and they are doted upon regularly by the hyenas who call themselves men. They only seek to prey upon younger women so that once they come of age, they know nothing but the man who *showed them love*. Today I come of age, and you want me to be devoted to you. You want me to believe you love me so that I will never betray you after tomorrow.

"But that is where you and the hyenas are mistaken." She looked up at him with a sorrowful shadow over her eyes. "You will never control us. We see your love as false and we cling to you because you give us what is made more difficult for us because we are women. All the while, we have the power. You know it and so do I. Reissgard is the last of the patriarchal empires left standing. Soon it too shall crumble as Astoria's has. When that happens, my marriage to you will serve as a reminder of who the one with true strength is. Perhaps then I will know real love. I will know what it is to be cared for."

"What do you know of true love, Ara—"

"I have told you not to speak my name before it is necessary to do so. It sounds like filth on your lips. I have seen it. In the Barrows when a mother looks to protect her child from would-be thieves. In the heights, when I saw the wedding of the two noblemen from that shoddy little city in the south. I also see it in my dreams. As though they were memories. Someone who stood over me and never failed to show me how much they truly loved me. Someone who reminded me of... regardless, that is how I know what you offer is false, however valuable it may be to me."

"Bite your tongue, girl." Cade stepped around the table. "Remember who runs things around here."

The witch smiled. She matched his stride until they met in the center of the room. She looked up into his eyes and placed her hand on his chest. Her palm began to glow white and her smile stretched further.

"From the moment I learned what I was, you never had any power over me."

Cade grit his teeth and stood his ground. The witch laughed softly as steam rose from his shirt. He grabbed her wrist and wrenched her hand away. He stumbled, grunted, and looked down at the hand-shaped burn in the center of his chest.

"Do you understand now?" she asked.

He had no words, but his glare spoke volumes. The low growl in his throat amused her. She reached out to run her finger across the vein pulsing in his neck, but he swatted her hand. She laughed again and turned her back to him.

"Come tomorrow I am done with the killing for sport. I'm sick of the bloodshed. You may use me as a threat, but I am no longer your weapon."

"You insolent—"

"I've seen the way the nobles in the other regions live. It's peaceful." She glided to the door and spoke with a soft whisper. "I'd like to try that."

20

Bonds

The night following their arrival at the Alchemy Guild sent Magnus and Elias into a spiral. Elias could not take his eyes off his father. He looked for words where there were none, but his father, Elijah, did not seem keen on giving him any hints. The words escaped Elias's lips only once and they were met with a simple shake of Elijah's head and the empty promise of *later.*

Magnus faced his own demons in the furthest corner of the guild house that he could find. Cade was close. He was closer than he had been in the last sixteen years. Meditation was the only thing that kept Magnus from running out of the front door and bursting through the Emerald Blood guild house with nothing but his fists and a death wish. Even meditation only worked for a short time. The longer he closed his eyes, the more he began to see the faces of phantoms — his wife, Boram, and all the fallen guards.

They had whispered to him endlessly over the last few days when the short rest on their trip gave him little energy and the world became a blur. They spoke of justice. They spoke of life. They spoke of death and they spoke of vengeance. He believed little in spirits, but he knew what their words were. They were echoes of his own thoughts. They were voices from his memories that reminded him of what he wished for.

He wondered if this was what he was meant to become. When he joined the guard, he was reaching towards the father that had vanished on him. He wanted to step closer to him despite whatever great distance lay between their paths. He wanted to be righteous, but now he only felt bloodlust. It terrified him to think that he would become what he sought to vanquish.

The only other wall between him and his lament was Neoma. During their journey to Reissgard, she was the only thought in his mind that did not tie him to Cade. The bandages on her face did nothing to detract from her ferocity or her presence. He knew she was also struggling with everything that had been lost, but somehow, she managed to focus on lifting him throughout the ordeal. He couldn't help but wonder if he deserved what she had given him.

He pushed himself up from the basement floor and crept up the stairs into the main hall. He walked through a large set of ornate wooden doors and made his way out onto the balcony overlooking the lower levels of the city. Ember was perched on the railing, looking at the hustle of the citizens below with shadows hanging over her eyes.

"I suppose it's not really a wonderous view from up here, is it?" Magnus asked.

"It used to be. From the Heights, the Barrows and the

Shelf always shone vibrantly, before he got here. They had celebrations in the street almost every night."

"What were they celebrating?"

"Life." She gestured for him to join her and pointed off into the distance. "You see that bodega down there in the Barrows?"

Magnus peered over the edge and did his best to make out the faraway shapes. He followed her finger until he saw what she spoke of. A small bodega carved from stone that was boarded up and covered with what looked to be the marks of small groups of thieves and vandals.

"That used to be my brother's shop. It was the only place in all of Reissgard where you could purchase Theldenian wine. My brother married a woman from a nomadic tribe and her family would pass by every few months and bring him crates of the stuff. No one else, not even the richest guilds, could get the stuff." Magnus could see the sad smile on her face.

"What happened?"

"The Emerald Blood hated that he wouldn't hand over a percentage of his inventory whenever he got it. He beat down so many of their members for trying to strongarm him that eventually, they went after him in other ways."

"They attacked the tribe, didn't they? Cut off the trade route."

"How do you figure?" Ember asked.

"It's what I would do if I were trying to stop a black-market trade ring. You spend enough time using certain tactics against criminals, they will develop their own use of the same methods. The line between justice and crime is rarely how something is done, but why you do it in the first place."

"I suppose I can agree with that. Both sides kill. Both sides steal. Both sides hold people against their will. Both sides lie."

"It's hard to say who's right these days. You can only do what your heart deems necessary." Magnus sighed. His breathing felt heavier than usual.

Ember turned and hopped down from the railing. Her feet landed with a soft *thud* on the balcony. She walked to the door with her hands dangling at her side and her head turned towards the sky.

"We've pretty much exhausted every diplomatic option there is."

"Even at its worst, would you not prefer to avoid war within your own city?" Magnus turned to face her. Her back was still to him, but he could tell there was a sad smile on her face even if he couldn't see it.

"We're already at war," she answered. "The real question is... who will end it?"

Ember walked through the door and into the hallway before Magnus could speak again. He looked up to see Elias and Neoma staring at him through the open doorway. Their faces lacked expression, but he could sense the worry emanating from them both. He was certain they'd heard the latter part of his conversation with Ember. They stepped over the threshold and joined him against the railing. In silence, they looked over the remains of a once-great city. The images conjured visions of home, or rather the place they'd once called home.

"They were waiting for you, Magnus. There's only one way that they expect this to end," Elias said, breaking the long quiet that hung between them.

"I'm unsure I can achieve what they expect of me. If we go

to battle now, even with everyone behind me, he just may be too powerful for me to defeat."

"I'm not so certain of that." Elias turned to face him. His eyes were narrowed with stern conviction beyond what Magnus and Neoma expected. "I have watched you for years. Whether you were aware or not."

"That's quite disturbing."

"Quiet, fool. What I mean is that I have seen your strength throughout my time in the city. Your tales of grandeur are often accompanied by abundant grandstanding, but most of what you speak of is true. When I find myself deployed to ensure the success of certain missions, I have witnessed you singlehandedly take on hordes of powerful men and women."

"And yet I failed to defeat him before."

"Because you give Cade the one thing you have refused to give any of your other opponents."

"What could you possibly mean?"

"Your fear," Neoma answered. "You face your other opponents without worry or hesitation, but Cade has weakened you by making you fear his strike before he raises his fist. Fear may keep us alive, but if we do not control it, we may also be crippled by it."

"So, it is my own weakness that will lose me the battle."

"Fear is not a weakness of the strong. It's what keeps us alive."

Magnus chuckled. He looked over at the sincere smile spread on Neoma's face and the confusion twisted on Elias's. He sighed, taking in the advice he once gave out and realized his own hypocrisy. His eyes dropped to his hands. They were calm. The worst of his sickness seemed to pass while he was unaware. He glanced at his companions and felt a flutter in his chest.

Elias was full of expression and compassion. A man Magnus once saw as a threat was now someone he could turn his back to and feel guarded. He was a friend and perhaps he had always trusted him in some way, but he was fixated on the title, rather than the man. They were so alike. Mirror images of a man with nothing to lose but their life.

When Magnus's eyes fell on Neoma, he truly knew that life had changed while he was blinded and unaware. He no longer saw the feisty apprentice whose skill with a blade was as unrefined as his own manner. He saw strength. He saw grace. He saw solidarity and stability. He saw the woman she had become. Perhaps the one she always was. He saw the warrior. In that moment — fleeting as it may have been — when he thought to call out for the one he loved, the name that seemed to flow through his mind and nearly spill from his lips was not Alandriel.

"What have we become?" The only words he could speak out loud. "One might not imagine the three of us could stand about this balcony and share in this moment beneath this blackened night. Yet here we are, having stared into death and daring to stare into the eyes of the reaper once more, together as one."

Elias cocked his eyebrow and glanced at Neoma. "Perhaps Magnus did perish on that battlefield and some wicked shapeshifter has taken his place. Because if I'm not mistaken, that bit of poetry was that of an intelligent man."

"Yes, it was also not his own. Ferian York if I'm not mistaken. A poet from Illyori during the Age of Minstrels some hundred years ago." Neoma spoke her words with pointed laughter.

Magnus shrugged, joining both Elias and Neoma in their amusement. They felt at peace in that moment. The pressure of their journey had long since coiled tightly around and threatened to suffocate them, but in their laughter, they found freedom from its grip. Aware as they were, that it would not last — that the memory of their fallen comrades and the injuries they had suffered on this difficult journey would swell in their minds and pierce their chest — they enjoyed this fleeting night and shared their joyous mood until they retired to their rooms for the night.

21

A Leader Shall Rise

The morning was filled with laughter and the sounds of clinking glasses and the ringing of cutlery before Magnus had opened his eyes. The joyous noise swept throughout the compound and set him adrift into the hallways to locate its source. The closer he crept, the more he became certain that ancestors long past could feel the rattle of the celebration in the afterlife.

The source, the dining hall just past the entrance of the guildhall, was alive with wonder. The members of the Alchemy Guild dug fervently into their breakfasts while dancing and singing about the room. Magnus stood in the doorway and watched as they let their spirit fill the room. Their energy intoxicated one another without fail. He could feel the swirl of emotions spilling out of them. He felt their deep sadness and their fears, but he also felt their hope and their love for one another. None of it was fake. None of it overtook the other. He couldn't help but smile as he stepped into the dining hall and basked in their merriment.

"Come, Magnus," Elijah called from the head table across the room. Elias and Neoma sat with him, along with Ember and a man that Magnus did not recognize. "Join us here so that we may discuss our plans for the day."

Magnus met his invitation with a nod and sauntered over to the head table. He took his seat next to Neoma. He looked over at the stranger sitting next to Elijah and felt the curious glance burning a hole into his mind. There was no malice, but a strong sense of wonder. He could feel him prying inside his head, looking to figure out who the man that had just joined the head table of his beloved guild was.

"If you care to know so deeply about me, it takes little more than a question," Magnus stated.

"My apologies," the man said, "I often find it to be much faster to look into the mind in order to understand the people I encounter. I tend to forget that such an invasion of privacy is considered rude amongst strangers and close friends alike."

Elijah clapped his hands together and smiled wistfully. "I forgot that you had not met last evening. Berol was off on assignment and only returned this morning. Magnus, Elias, and Neoma, this is Berol Winterlin, my second in command and Reissgard's chief informant. He serves as a central information hub for the majority of Reissgard's populace."

"For a price of course," Berol added.

"Pleasure to meet you, Berol." Magnus outstretched his hand.

Berol waited for a moment, smiled, then shook Magnus's hand with surprisingly graceful refinement. His motions were fluid and dignified; something Magnus often only saw in the nobility of Astoria and Illyori. When Berol leaned back in his chair that was when Magnus noticed that all of his movements seemed to have a flow to them that denoted royalty in his upbringing, but his appearance was more of a barbarian — rather someone who spent a large portion of their life amidst battlefields.

Magnus couldn't help but be intrigued by the puzzling features of the man. His arms were toned and rigid, covered with marks that told stories of his past, whether it be ink or scars. His clothing was torn to display the art that covered most of his body and his posture seemed to present his muscular frame to the forefront for all to see. His face was angular and adorned with numerous piercings and baubles that looked as though the slightest movement would entangle them in the mane that wrapped around his chin. All of this framed by a cascading bunch of dreaded hair spilling from the top of his head and down his back. He was a mountainous man whose graceful movements betrayed his appearance.

"You're absolutely correct." Berol answered Magnus's thoughts with a wicked smile. He leaned forward on the table, causing it to shift slightly beneath his weight. "I was once a noble of Illyori, highborn into a disastrous family of thieves and courtesans. We made our money off the wickedness of man and after some time I found it was not the place where I felt at home. Though this was long after their lessons were ingrained into my personality."

Neoma and Elias looked between them with raised brows.

"Answering a question set within one's mind leaves little context for those without your capabilities or their thoughts, Berol." Elijah raised his arm and placed a powerful hand across the back of Berol's head. The *pop* of the impact echoed through the hall, despite the cushion Berol's hair must have provided.

Berol laughed as he rubbed the back of his head. He grinned bashfully and looked up at Elijah as though this were far too common an occurrence. "My apologies once again. Minds flow to me as simply as one's speech. I tend to forget the two."

"Nevertheless, I'm happy that you are all here so that we can discuss our preparations for today and be ready to finish Cade's tyranny tomorrow." Elijah slid his plate from in front of him and placed his elbows where it had been. He rested his chin upon his interlocked fingers and heaved a heavy sigh. "Not facing issues head-on by my own strength is often troubling for me, but over the recent years, I have had to put much more on these young people in order to get jobs done. Though I haven't known you long, I do find that I must ask the same of you, Magnus, if I am to see Reissgard returned to its former self."

"What is it that you would ask of me?"

"Before I explain, I must ask, are you all familiar with Reissgard's governing system?"

"Somewhat," Neoma answered, "unlike Astoria and Illyori's monarchies, Reissgard consists of a council of guild leaders that act as the governing body. Laws and regulations are determined by popular vote and debate by the council, correct?"

"Yes, that is correct. The High Council is formed by the top six guilds, led by the masters of those guilds. The even number allows us the opportunity for ties in votes which brings about debates that are normally civilized and lead to at least one person shifting their vote so that we can determine how Reissgard will be affected. This has worked well over a great many years since Reissgard's inception. Being the third of the four kingdoms to form, we are still quite young, but our governing system has been noted as one of the most efficient amongst the four kinds present in Aévan."

"Until recently, our own was considered the worst. A hereditary monarchy with a single person holding absolute power. Unlike Illyori's which is determined by selection, the Ahlvadrian hold significant power along with the king's decisions. Even as the two oldest kingdoms our governing systems are often called into question because they are easily influenced by the whims of a single person."

"The two of you know far more about governing systems than I do," Magnus interjected.

"I hear ya," Ember added.

"Imbeciles," Elijah whispered.

"Nevertheless, your description is exact, Neoma. Governing bodies led by a single person gives rise to tyrannical leadership. Thus, the current situation in Illyori. Their kingdom is under immense distress over the actions of their most recent king. This is why the situation in Reissgard is so detrimental and why the guilds were often kept in check, so their power balance never shifted too suddenly and without limit."

"It was Cade who undermined that balance when he snuck onto the council by hiding the true strength of his guild." Berol's kind features turned sour as Cade's name rolled off his tongue. "He hid the witch, along with his true name, before challenging Master Elijah for his seat on the council. This challenge, that which we call *Maesir Amdama*, is bound by law once a victor has been decided. It was after winning this bout that Cade revealed the true level of his power and the name of his guild. By then it was too late. He had cemented his influence in Reissgard, and none could stand to stop him."

"Could the guilds not come together and drive him from the kingdom?" Magnus asked.

"Perhaps we could, but the precedent it would set would be unsettling. What if another decided that they wanted to remove another council member from their seat after Cade was gone? They could simply offer money, treasures, or the vacant seat on the council to whoever joined them. Whether their promises were true or not, the damage would be done. Our system is not without its flaws, but it has worked, and we do actively strive to improve." Elijah gave his words with confidence, but the weariness in his gaze told Magnus that he likely asked the same question to someone who had given him the answer he regrettably repeats now.

"At first, we still had hope," Elijah continued, "but it did not last. When Cade wanted to push his agenda, the threat of the witch's power swayed the other council members to vote in his favor. Soon, his proposals were less that, and more suited to be called absolute orders. With each one, the Emerald Blood's influence grew, and Reissgard fell to ruin. He turned the entire kingdom into his own safehouse. Somewhere his enemies around Aévan would not dare touch him without the threat of war between the four kingdoms breaking out. Even if he ventured out of the city walls, killing him—"

"Would be an attack against Reissgard. If it happened and the other members of the council did not retaliate, it would make Reissgard look weak. His plans were well thought out. Even his death would bring misery to the realm." Berol grit his teeth. His hands clenched so tight that blood dripped from his palms.

"I imagine that none were able to defeat him in order to regain their seat. Which must be where I come in." Magnus peered over his interlocked fingers with a vicious glare.

"Yes. Over the years, our spies have ascertained a single weakness in the beast of the Emerald Blood. His vendetta with you. Every other action he takes is meticulous and devastating, but you seem to be the only blind spot he has. For you, he feels nothing but rage, and that makes his discussion and planning falter to a small, exploitable degree."

"Yet, there seems to be a single flaw in your plan. Even if I were to form a guild, I have no wish to sit on the Reissgardian council. My defeating him would only put me at odds with the other members."

"A trivial matter. A member of the council can willingly give up their seat if they so choose. They must only relinquish their title as guild master. So, I am not asking you to form your own guild, Magnus. I am asking you to take the title of Guild Master of the Alchemy Guild and remove Cade by way of the *Maesir Amdama*."

"Are you certain that this is the course of action you wish to take? What of your men? Will they not oppose a stranger taking this title? If I were not a man with whom you could place your trust, giving me this title could give me the opportunity to do significant damage to your guild."

"The fact that you would state that so boldly shows me that I have nothing to fear. If my son trusts you, then so shall

I. If you are concerned about my men, then we can simply ask them" With those words, Elijah turned to Berol and nodded.

Berol pushed his chair out and stood in front of the dining hall. With a deep breath, his chest widened, and a monstrous roar escaped his throat. The entire hall fell to silence in an instant and every member turned and faced the head table. Elijah stood before them with his arms outstretched as though he was embracing them all. None of their eyes lingered elsewhere. They watched him closely, waiting for his word.

"Brothers and sisters of the Alchemy Guild, long have we lived under the thumb of a tyrant. Today I offer a solution. One I have utmost faith in. If we are able to exploit Cade's weakness and regain the seat which we have lost on the council, then we can bring peace and civility back to our beloved home. To do so, I aim to hand my title as Guild Master over to this man." He gestured to Magnus. Magnus stood up and looked out at the crowd whose eyes all shifted in his direction. "Magnus Alexander is someone who can remove Cade from our home and help us restore our home. So, I ask you, my guild, my family, will you put your faith in me, in him, as the one to lead us forward?"

Magnus looked out, expecting some words or someone to question this statement, but his eyes widened, and his jaw dropped when he saw the guild's response. Every member turned to face him. Together, without saying a single word, they slammed an arm across their chest and saluted Magnus. Each of their faces was stern. There was no question about his motives or distrust in their hearts emanating from them. Magnus felt all of their fears drift away and there was nothing left but faith. Faith and hope in the man that was presented to them as their new leader, even if it was only to take down Cade.

"This is the Alchemy Guild, Magnus. For as long as you see fit, even after you defeat Cade tomorrow, we are yours to lead. In you, we have absolute faith."

Elijah, Berol, and Ember turned to Magnus and saluted him. Magnus looked out over the crowd in front of him and he couldn't believe what he was seeing. He was terrified that once again, he might disappoint those who now relied on him, but he was also invigorated. He could feel their trust in him, and for the first time in sixteen years, he felt that he could win.

22

About a Blade

The rest of the day after their breakfast feast was relatively calm. Guild members went to the training halls and sparred. Magnus sat and watched for some time, his eyes scanning their every move. Some of them impressed him. Most of them were like him. They took their stance without armor and wielded their fists with the confidence of a pro. Their movements were slower than his own, but they were no less precise. No less lethal if they intended to kill their opponent.

Others bore more resemblance to Neoma, though it was not only swords brandished in the atrium. Lances, staffs, spears, and daggers swirled and slashed through the air as the fighters danced around one another. He knew that they were different from Astoria. They had no guard and no army — only guilds. They were the defining element of Reissgard's entire structure, but to see so many variations, whether they wore armor or not, was still impressive in such a confined space. Somehow each of them seemed to have a mastery over their preferred art, but their skill levels were so similar, it was difficult to distinguish who among them taught the others.

Only one stood out from the crowd. A woman who was most certainly the one who taught others how to wield twin daggers. Her movements were like Neoma's — agile, with no wasted efforts. Her fighting was something that truly mirrored a dance one might see in a festival. While Neoma's sword dance was a spectacle that should not be forgotten, this woman's was different. Her battle dance was more refined and elegant. While Neoma's dance was modernistic, hers was classical — something one would see in a production crafted in the Age of the Bard.

She stood between four of her students and took her stance. It was a sight just to see that much; Her foot sliding about her as though it glided through the air. Her core tightened, strengthened so that her muscles could prepare. Her arms twirled into position with grace, and when they were ready, they were like snakes ready to strike. He could see the structure. What movements she might make to defend — to attack. Her students lacked her composure but made up for it in technique. Their stances were solid, firm, yet afforded them the mobility one seeks with the dagger.

When the fight began Magnus could not blink, nor look away. If a ballad had begun to play, her dance would enrich the melody. She parried their strikes, swam beneath their torrent of slashes, and turned an outnumbered bout into a one-sided display of martial prowess. It was not to say the others showed no skill. They were simply, undeniably, outclassed in every way. Her movements bewitched them. They made no moves that she did not foresee. *No.* He thought to himself. He was wrong. Every strike was commanded by her — her own and her opponents'. She did not have to predict what she induced.

When the last of her students hit the ground with a resounding *thud*, Magnus pushed off the wall and trotted to her battleground. "Teach me."

The woman looked up and wiped the sweat from her brow, a playful smile drawn across her lips. "The new Guild Master, giving orders only a few hours in. Impressive."

"My apologies." Magnus cleared his throat, feeling embarrassed by his own impolite approach. "Magnus, Magnus Alexander. Perhaps before being so upfront I should have asked your name."

"Can't very well fault you, can I? You are the man in charge. We all agreed to follow you, don't forget that. My given name is Freyr. My family is shit, so I dropped that name."

"Well, it's a pleasure to meet you Freyr. Suffice to say, your talent in combat is remarkable. Where did you train?"

Freyr's gaze drifted off to the side. Her chest heaved and a deep sigh escaped her lungs. "Cystrian."

"Cystrian? I've never heard of that school. Is it native to Reissgard?"

"It's not a school. It's a troupe." Her words came out muted and unclear.

"Troop? As in military training?"

"No." She sighed again and lifted her sleeve to show the tattoo on her wrist. It was the abbreviation CST atop what looked like a ball. "The Cystrian Troupe. As in performance troupe. I was a knife thrower and a blade dancer."

"I see. It's an unusual background, but your skills are far more refined than simple performance."

"They weren't for a long time. I came here and things changed. I turned my performance style into a martial art. So, what you see is actual dancing, but now my blade is meant for blood, not just entertainment."

"Regardless of its origins, you did something that captivated me. It was as though your moves led your opponents, rather than your dodge being reactionary. I was hoping you would show me how you did that."

"It's not something you pick up in a day. It's also not something one person could teach you. Every weapon and every stance has its own strikes and movements. When you know what these are, you often know what your opponent is going to do based on your own position. So, I think two steps ahead. I place myself in a position and draw out the attack I know they are going to execute. Once an attack is in motion, it's often difficult to stop."

"So, you're not reacting. You're the puppeteer. I've never heard of something so intricate. The amount of knowledge something like that would require is monumental."

"The troupe traveled throughout Aévan year-round. I saw many schools and many Ahndaele. Even styles that are new to me often have similar tactics to others I have studied. They can be manipulated as long as I err on the side of caution."

"I understand why you say it can't be taught so easily. I won't bother you anymore about it." Magnus gave Freyr a quick salute and turned to leave the training hall.

"Hey, Guild Master," Freyr called out, "you might not be able to learn the full technique, but you have an advantage.

Cade is quick to anger and more so when you're involved. Anger is blinding in battle and when there's a personal stake, manipulating your opponent becomes as simple as goading them on. So, use that, but be careful on your part as well."

"Of course. I lost to him once. I know what he is capable of."

"That's not what I meant. Yes, you can use his anger, but he can also use yours. He's a brute, but he's clever. Don't let him manipulate you. If he does, we all lose." With that, she returned his salute and went back to the circle of guild members she sparred with earlier.

Magnus stared at her back as they prepared for another match. Her words echoed in his mind, but he wasn't sure how strongly he could heed her warning. She was right. Cade had been under his skin just as much as he was under Cade's.

He turned again and left the hall. His legs felt heavy and his mind clouded. He turned through the twisted halls without care where his feet led him. He passed by various guild members, but their faces became a blur as his mind focused more and more on the battle he would face tomorrow. He'd wished for this day for so long that he never realized that he might not be prepared for it when it came. Now that it was here, it was the only thing on his mind.

When he looked up from the floor, he was out on the balcony again. In front of him was Neoma. She looked out over the city, unaware of his presence. He watched her in silence for a moment. One hand caressed the bandaged side of her face while the other curled into a fist. Her frustration drifted off her and into him. He walked up beside her and placed his hand on top of hers.

"It seems you have been far more affected than you let us know."

"It's not just hurt for now. Yeseni tried to heal it, but the damage was done. My eye is gone. Along with my abilities. As it is now, I'm simply a swordsman." She grit her teeth and pounded her fist on the railing.

"Simply? What is simple about your skill with a blade. What makes you inferior to another? You are far from simple. You just may well be the greatest swordsman I have ever encountered."

"Your words are honeyed, yet they remain bitter. My advantage on the battlefield was my ability. Without it..." She hung her head. The sound of her tears on the stone beneath their feet sent a chill through Magnus. Her wave of sorrow crashed on him and his body became heavier with her sadness.

"You lost one. Only one."

Neoma looked up at him with her eyebrow raised. Magnus wiped the tears from her eyes and stared down at her. His face was stern and serious. Neoma recoiled at the severity of his gaze.

"You lost only one ability," Magnus continued. "You have far more than your eye. You had talent. You refined that with training. You honed your blade in battle and your knowledge of the battlefield is far beyond your years. You have seen tragedy and faced it head-on. That is your strength. That is your ability. The strength to keep going. Nobody can take that from you."

"How are you so sure? How can you have more faith in me than I have in myself?"

"Because I was weak," he replied. He grabbed the hand

that was curled into a fist and placed the other on her cheek. "When I had given up on the world, when I was ready to let the days take me and rot alive, that strength is what you gave me. I might never have had the confidence to make it here if it were not for you. You gave me my life back by simply being you. It was not your eye that made you a warrior. It was not your eye that pushed you through the ranks and made you the youngest captain the Royal Guard has ever seen. You did that on your own. Abilities are tools. They are not who we are. Never forget that."

Neoma's breathing was heavy and her face was warm. Her eyes darted between Magnus's eyes and his lips. Her palm started to sweat, and she suddenly became aware of just how dry her throat was. She couldn't form the words she wanted to say in her mind and all she could reply was, "You're incredibly close right now."

Magnus chuckled and stroked her cheek with his thumb. "When this is all over. After I defeat Cade and hand the guild back over to Elijah... marry me."

Neoma inhaled sharply and her eyes widened. "If you die on me tomorrow. I swear to the ancestors I will carve you to pieces."

"That was an absolutely terrifying way to respond to that." Magnus leaned forward and pressed his lips against hers. He felt the clouds in his mind drift away and the weight in his body seemed to disappear all at once.

They stood there for what felt like an eternity. The night air seemed warmer than it had a moment ago and the city much farther away. They had no intention of releasing their coiled embrace until they heard the footsteps tapping around the corner. They pulled apart slowly and smiled as they looked into each other's eyes once more before turning to see who impeded on their moment. Elias stood in the doorway. He leaned against the frame with a sideways smile on his face.

"I was almost ready to give up on you two. Though to be fair, I was certain she would have made a move first. Seems you're bolder than I expected *jyulmain.*"

"Will you ever stop calling me that?" Magnus asked.

"Once the pieces are picked up and you're put back together, then it will no longer apply." Elias shrugged and stepped out onto the balcony next to them.

"Is there a particular reason that you have joined us, Elias?" Neoma's tone was friendly, but the words had an edge that was undeniable.

"Well, it seems that my father is still Astorian at heart. He sent me to fetch you and bring you to the dining hall. A feast has been prepared and there seems to be enough wine to intoxicate an entire village."

"I suppose celebration is never bad before facing one's potential death. It's no surprise the guild is not opposed to such a tradition," Magnus said.

"Well, our upcoming battle is not the only thing to celebrate it seems. I did hear the whole thing."

"Just how long were you standing there?" Neoma asked.

"Just about at, 'you're incredibly close right now.'" He mimicked her heavy breathing and flustered tone then let out a raspy laugh.

"You won't be there for the wedding if you're dead, Elias. Remember that the next time you mock me." Neoma stomped her foot in front of him and Elias threw his hands up in surrender.

"Yeah, yeah. I hear ya. Let's get to the dining hall before they get into the full swing of things. We'll raise a toast, to the two of you. This journey has taught me a lot."

"Well, it's not over yet. Still one more thing to do," Neoma muttered.

"We'll take down Cade. Of that I no longer have any doubt," Magnus said.

"What of your daughter? Has anyone brought you any news?" Elias asked.

"Not yet, but I feel her. I felt her in Grithala and then again when we got into town. Now that I know Cade was there too, I know he's kept her close. I'm certain she's alive. I'll bring her home. No matter what."

23

Black Wedding

Cade stared into the tarnished glass and observed his image with care. His clothes were finely tailored, and it was almost uncomfortable for him to be in something he wouldn't wear on any normal occasion. He grasped at the tie dangling around his neck and snarled at the reflection looking back at him.

"I will never understand how those noble wretches dress in such a fashion every day. How constricting can one's clothing be?"

His words filled the empty room and echoed back into his mind. Once he was straightened up to his own standards, he kicked open the door that led into the hallway and stomped through the corridor until he reached the atrium of the council building. The rest of the Emerald Blood, along with a few of the citizens he'd forced to come, stood about the space surrounding their matrimony arch. Miryllyn stood below the floral structure and shifted back and forth on her heels as he approached. The room fell silent when he came into view and the other members of the council glared in his direction.

A vicious smile crossed his lips. He took the hatred in stride and felt joyous that so many people opposed his marriage to the witch. Every person that detested this marriage was one he could leverage. Her loyalty would become so deeply cemented in their eyes that all their scheming to turn her would be for naught.

Yet Cade still had his own misgivings about the marriage he placed upon himself. With all his power and all that he gave her throughout her entire life, he'd grown to detest who she was. He wanted nothing more than her power. A power that was meant to be his before it was stolen. Now he had to use it by other means, and she was difficult to control. If not for her own selfish desires, he might have killed her in her sleep and started anew.

Once he stood beneath the arch, next to Miryllyn, two women from his guild rushed to the opposite end of the hall and through another set of doors where the witch awaited her entrance. All eyes were on the door and a few moments later, she emerged.

A collective gasp filled the room when she came into view. For the first time, everyone could see just how beautiful the witch they all feared truly was. Her raven-colored hair was curled and pinned in an elegant manner that resembled the highest of royals. The ends that spilled from the top and down to her shoulders were dyed white which contrasted wondrously against her dark skin. Her makeup was soft and only served to accent the vibrant gold of her eyes and frame her face so that she looked to be a flawless portrait turned mortal.

As though her appearance was not astonishing enough, the dress she wore put the richest women of Reissgard to shame. The luminous silk of her red dress shone beautifully in the sunlight that streamed through the high arching windows of the grand hall. Every step she took caused the lacey texture of her adornments to shimmer and send a wave of adoration through the onlookers. No one could take their eyes off her.

This appalled her. She hated their stares and she grit her teeth to hold back from lashing out. She knew what they thought of her and the adornments could not so easily sway their judgements. All of this was mere pageantry. The dress, the hair, the wedding as a whole was a show for their amusement. Cade pushed the idea that everything had to be as real and flawless as possible, but in their pursuit of authenticity, everything had been faked. Her feelings, her position, and even the vows she wrote contained her authentic feelings, but she had to lie about who they were intended for. When she looked up at Cade, standing beneath the arch, she only thought of sending a bolt straight through his heart.

Despite her anger, she stepped beneath the arch and played her part. Miryllyn's eyes darted between the two of them. She felt as though she were nothing more than a thin wall between two powerful weapons ready to fire upon one another. She could feel their animosity and her heart beat faster with each passing second. She took a deep breath, looked out at the crowd of people staring up at them, and began the ceremony.

"We have gathered here today, before the eyes of our ancestors to recognize this bond of matrimony." Her voice cracked and echoed throughout the hall. "We recognize this bond as a symbol of promises made and the strength of the love shared between these two people. In order to complete this bond, we ask that you, Cade, and you, Aramecia, share your promises with your beloved before the eyes of the ancestors. In doing so, may they be blessed by their favor."

"Ladies first," Cade whispered with a mocking grin.

The witch, Aramecia, clicked her tongue then took a deep breath before reciting the words she'd written. "I have spent my entire life wishing for a family and wishing to feel what love really was. I have dreamt and envisioned how it would feel to be embraced without judgement and without intent, except to be cared for. So, with this, I vow to you, that I will uphold our bond with honesty and devotion."

Aramecia clicked her tongue again and felt a deep disgust as she spoke the words to Cade. She felt her truth soured with every word she uttered. Then she felt sadness. Without ever feeling a need to lie, she could not write vows she felt were untrue. Her heart felt heavy that the words she spoke would never be true when the sun set on her wedding day. And when Cade opened his mouth to speak, she wished that she could strike him down without a second thought.

* * *

Magnus stood in front of the Alchemy Guild and took in their fervor for battle. Despite how he felt, looking into the sea of intensity that stared back into him changed his perspective of what this was about. They were ready to fight, just as much, if not more than he was, but their blades and their fist were carried by a want, a need for freedom. It was in this that he put his trust. When he looked down at his hands, he could no longer sense the warrior he once was.

There was a time where all he wanted was justice. He wanted to be strong so that he could protect those around him but looking at them made him realize that he had not been protecting anyone. This was his first real chance to use his strength for something outside of himself. Even if revenge had brought him here, it wasn't what would help him win. He could see that. He could feel it just as powerfully as he felt their emotions float up to him. Yet he still found it difficult not to wish for Cade's head. Even if it were only to fulfill his own justice.

He stepped closer to the assembled guild members and took a deep breath before he spoke. "Today you all put your faith in me so I will give back that much and more to you. Sixteen years ago, this man took everything I had. Then he came here, and he took your home away from you. After today, he will take nothing more. Today, we teach him and his guild what it means to be defeated. We will teach them what it means to be the ones without power!"

The guild erupted with cheers. The walls shook with their anticipation and Magnus was energized by them. He stepped down from the raised platform and walked through the crowd of guild members before him. He pushed through the front doors and led them out into the streets of Reissgard. Elijah, Elias, Neoma, and Ember walked beside him. Their faces were stern and full of anger. All of it directed towards the towering council hall on the city level above them.

The guild marched in an unorganized parade. The common people of the city cheered their advance. The news of

Cade's wedding had reached all their ears and the force that stomped through the city streets was welcomed by all. Not one of them turned away or slid into the shadows to avoid what was to come. Instead, they pushed them higher. They walked alongside them and gave every member all their hopes and prayers. Magnus was overwhelmed by what he felt from them. For the first time, every person around him was actively feeling something, the same thing, so strong that it nearly blinded him.

They pressed on, pushing through the gates to the upper level, and marched up to the front door of the council building. A dozen Emerald Blood members stood out front with their weapons drawn. Their feet were planted, and their faces showed no fear, and yet they reeked of it. Ember stepped forward along with a handful of Alchemy's members.

"Go on ahead, Guild Master. We'll join you in a second. I don't think I can wait any longer." A crooked grin spread across Ember's face. She pounded her fist into her palm, sending sparks out of her hand.

Magnus nodded. He walked forward, ignoring the Emerald Blood thug charging at him with a pike. Ember swept her hands forward, sending him flying with a burst of flames. Unmoved, he and the rest of the guild walked through their line while their comrades kept them at bay. Magnus looked up at the massive ornate stone doors and put his hands against them. He pushed them open without hesitation.

Every body in the room shifted at once. Whispers filled the air, giving the massive space a sudden ghostly atmosphere. Magnus's eyes locked in on Cade with ease. The bandit guild leader stood under his matrimonial arch as though his presence there wasn't unusual or malicious. The witch stood beside him and Magnus was thrown by her looks. He stared at her and tears formed in his eyes, but he couldn't understand the surge of emotion he felt.

When she looked back at him, her face was devoid of emotion. She showed neither anger nor fear at the unwelcome arrival. All he sensed was annoyance. It wasn't focused, but it was strong. A feeling directed at every person in the room. Something else was behind it, but she hid it well. Like she could sense him digging into her heart and she was pushing back.

Magnus stumbled forward, but he couldn't take his eyes off of her. The wedding guests scrambled out of their seats and rushed towards the exit behind the Alchemy guildmembers that now filled the room.

"Beautiful, isn't she?" Cade's cold tone drew Magnus's attention once more.

"Quite. It makes me wonder how she could stomach marrying a snake such as you."

"Yes, well we all have our charms." His words were followed by a guttural laugh that the other Emerald Blood members in the room echoed in earnest. Everyone but the witch, who glanced over at Cade with disgust.

"Enough of the small talk, Cade. This is over. You've taken enough from these people. From everyone."

"Have I? You seem to think of me as the bad guy here, but am I not simply doing what every person here has done? I have the strength; thus, I have the power. What I've done is neither good nor evil. It's the natural order of the world. It's justice."

"You've terrorized this city with your power. You've taken everything from them. Just like you did to me." Magnus grit his teeth and stepped forward.

"I TOOK NOTHING FROM YOU!" Cade's screaming shook the room. "Everything you had was mine. Everything you loved was never yours to claim in the first place. You stole EVERYTHING from me. That is why I won't let you go about your life as though it has some false hope or meaning. That is why *I* will be the one to end your petty little existence. That is how this will end."

"I took from you? Have the years rotted that sick mind of yours? You murdered my wife. You left me half dead in a village you burned to the ground. Then you ripped my daughter from me and laughed in my face. How dare you accuse me of taking anything from you?"

"Did you ever ask yourself, why? Why I tracked you and that bitch to that pitiful little place at the foot of the mountains? Why, for the first time in years, the infamous Cade left the confines of the Wildlands to hunt some insignificant little guardsman?"

"I asked myself all of that for years. All I could come up with was that somewhere in your disgusting reasoning, it made sense to you. I would never feign to understand the mind of a psychopath. It's something I'd say I'm quite proud of. Not knowing how your mind works is probably the one thing redeeming me still. It reminds me that I am nothing like you."

"Perhaps that's the answer. Perhaps not. I would tell you to ask Alandriel," Cade whispered his next words, his lips twisting into a malicious grin, "but I crushed her throat right before I strung her up. Remember?"

A monstrous roar escaped Magnus's lungs as he lunged forward. Cade caught his fist and leaned into him. His breath was hot against Magnus's face. They pushed back and forth, trying to overpower the other. Magnus jumped and jammed both of his feet into Cade's abdomen, sending him stumbling backward.

"I hereby challenge you to an official *Maesir Amdama*. Do you accept?" Magnus called out as he picked himself up off the ground.

Cade clutched his stomach and smiled at him. "Happily."

"This won't end the same as last time. I'm done losing to you."

"We'll see about that." Cade turned to his guildmembers and barked his order. "Leave Magnus to me. Kill the rest."

The hall erupted in chaos. Almost every person in the room jumped into battle without a second thought. The Alchemy Guild versus the Emerald Blood. Blades clashed, blood was spilled, and abilities were launched from every corner of the room. The only one who stood still was the witch.

"What the hell are you doing?" Cade yelled. "Get to work!"

She shook her head and walked from beneath the arch. "No. This battle is your own. I told you before. I'm done fighting for you."

She started towards a door off the side of the room. Neoma leapt past Magnus and Cade and rushed her with a sword drawn. "Like hell I'd let you just walk away."

"I don't wish to fight with you." The witch dodged Neoma's

slashes with ease, but her movement was restricted in her dress and she fell backward.

"Where was that noble attitude when you burned my face? When you and your men slaughtered our people?" She placed her blade beneath the witch's chin.

"I don't know what it's like to care for another, so I don't know what you're feeling right now, but I was not the one who spilled the blood of your comrades. I may have burned your face, but had I not, would you not be dead?" The witch's face was devoid of emotion as she spoke, but even Neoma could tell that everything she said was true.

Tears born of frustration clouded her vision. "If you truly don't wish to spill blood then why do you align yourself with the Emerald Blood?"

"What else do I have?" The witch steadied herself and looked back into Neoma's eyes. "I've been offered money to betray them, but that would mean killing Cade. Perhaps the rest of the guild. The Emerald Blood raised me. For all their distrust, they rarely pay close attention to my action. So, I let them believe that I killed for their sake, but in truth... I've never taken a life. As long as I've been with them, I've had no need to spill blood, even if they asked me to. I only let them think that I had while they swung their swords and created their own chaos. I do not intend to take a life. I have found no reason I believed in strong enough to will me to do so. That being said, I have no intention to die here either. If you intend to pursue my life, then I have no choice but to fight back."

"Is that so?" Cade growled. "It seems I've been far too lenient with you."

Magnus dug his fist into Cade's cheek while he was distracted. "Are you surprised that not everyone is as blood-thirsty or monstrous as you? Face reality, Cade. Some people just want to live."

Cade grunted and retaliated. They were both skilled in hand-to-hand combat. Every strike was precise, but Cade's larger build gave him an advantage that Magnus lacked. His fist carried more weight and even through his guard, Magnus could feel the impact throughout his body.

He watched Cade closely and tried to find a weakness in his movements. Even with his larger build, he was just as quick as Magnus. He ducked punches and guarded kicks with ease. Even so, Magnus landed a few blows through his guard. Both of them stared each other down, panting, and dripping blood and sweat on the ground around them.

"What do you know of monsters boy?" Cade asked.

"I can recognize one when I see it."

"Can you? You shared your bed with a monster for years and yet here you are, trying to avenge the death of someone who was more of a beast than I'll ever be."

"What are you talking about? Why should I believe a word you say?"

"You wanted answers, right? About why I hunted you down? Answers about why I blame you? The answer is simple. It was never you. I only hated you. I *hunted* her."

Magnus lunged again. He swung out wildly at Cade. Cade laughed as he danced around every punch. Magnus became more frustrated with every jab that didn't connect. The longer they fought, the slower he felt himself becoming. He feinted with his left and jabbed at Cade's chest with his right. He missed again, but this time Cade wrapped his arm around

Magnus's and jammed his fist into Magnus's stomach. When Magnus doubled over from the pain, Cade grabbed the back of his head and slammed it down to meet his rising knee.

Magnus toppled backward, slamming into the ground. Blood poured from his nose and his vision blurred. His face felt hot and it took everything in him not to cry out from the pain swelling in his broken nose. His body convulsed while he struggled to push himself up from the floor. Cade pressed his foot on Magnus's chest and laughed at his injured opponent.

"Have you ever heard the rumors of the ghost fort in the Wildlands? A base in that stretch of land your smug little kingdoms call unclaimed territory, or No Man's Land, despite the fact that people, *my* people, have lived there since before Aévan was settled. There in that stretch of land is an experimental military base where Astoria and Illyori banded together to create the ultimate weapon. They wanted to find a way to artificially create witches. That's right. If they succeed, then they'd be able to muster an army of witches to take down any enemy they saw fit. And who of course would be the test subjects for this little experiment of theirs? That's right, the inhabitants of the Wild Lands: kids, elders, mothers, fathers. Anyone they thought would be strong enough to withstand the torture."

Magnus writhed on the ground and swung his arm to knock Cade's foot away. "What does that have to do with me? I don't know anything about that."

"Oh, you see it has everything to do with you. Who do you think runs such a place? It's not some plucky little nobody like you. When you want something that big guarded, you send your best. You send a soldier. You send the Mistress of Mercy. The word 'mercy' being utter bullshit of course. I can assure you, she showed none to the people they experimented on."

"Your lies will not sway me. Alandriel would never do something so sick."

"Oh, but you see, she did. If you wait till the end of my story, I'll even give you proof." He leaned down and tapped his hand on the side of Magnus's face. "You see, nobody is going to interrupt us. They're all fighting for their own lives. Even if they weren't, they can't help you, otherwise, your little challenge is all for nothing. But don't worry, you'll love how this little tale ends. In fact, you were there. Remember?

"Now, where was I? Ah, right. Your wife was a world-class bitch. A smart one though. You see, when they started construction on the base, she sought out someone in the Wildlands that she knew didn't give a shit about the wellbeing of the people. She needed someone with power who was out for themselves. Then, lo and behold, I appeared. The Mistress and the Emerald Blood worked hand in hand. It was the greatest partnership I could have asked for. I truly mean that. You see, the Mistress got quite lonely out there and she was not a fan of the other little Astorians and Illyorians that were out there playing soldier. So, once again she turned to me and wouldn't you believe it, we were two beasts in love. At least, that's what I thought. So, you can imagine my surprise when she leaves and, on her return, I'm told that we're done because she's fallen in love with some pitiable young upstart in the Royal Guard."

"I don't care for your stories!" Magnus mustered what strength he had left and kicked up from the ground. He placed a well-timed kick against the side of Cade's head and knocked him to the side.

Cade laughed and spit the blood that pooled in his mouth on the ground. "We're just getting to the good part though."

"You keep spilling this useless dribble, but I see no reason to believe anything you have to say. Where is your proof? If you're here, then that means they succeeded. I see no army of witches. Only one who clearly has no love for you." Magnus glanced over to where Neoma and the witch still stood, fighting a halfhearted battle.

"Well of course I left. My reason for being there ran away with the snake who stole her from me. Though you're right. The experiment should have been complete. In fact, it was. Up until Alandriel had a change of heart about what we had been up to. Only one serum was made. She stole it when she left. Along with the life of the alchemist who figured it all out and his notes. You see, that's the part that no one knew except for me. I mean how could I let that bit of information slip? They would have killed her before I got my hands on her."

"Alandriel wasn't a witch. Neither was anyone in Astoria. All you're doing is wasting my time."

"Right once again! I was curious as to why she didn't take the serum as well, so I asked her that night in Crowind. Guess what I discovered. She did. What she didn't know is that she was already pregnant at the time. She thought it simply didn't work and the alchemist got it all wrong, but you see, I saw the bigger picture. I was certain the serum worked, and I was right. So, my plans to kill the two of you and leave your little girl to the life of a pitiful orphan... evolved. I knew right then and there, I could have a witch of my own."

"You mean—" Magnus's eyes widened, and he turned his head.

"I'm surprised you couldn't tell. She really is the spitting image of her mother."

Cade's words were louder than he intended. The witch heard every word. Magnus could feel her hatred boil inside her, stronger than it was before, and all of it was directed to him. She turned her head and glared at him with vicious bloodlust. A powerful wave of energy burst out of her, knocking everyone in the room off their feet. Her screams echoed throughout the hall and shook the members of both guilds to their core.

She stomped over to Cade and lifted him to his feet, holding him in place with her power. "You murdered my mother. You let me spend my entire life thinking that my family was killed because of me. Because of what I am!"

Magnus stood up slowly with his eyes locked on Aramecia. The room was silent. All eyes were on them now.

"Don't," Magnus spoke up. "I understand your rage, better than anyone else here, but this battle is mine."

"Magnus Alexander. If I had known... I wouldn't have—"

"We'll figure this out later. I promise you, but right now, this battle is bigger than us."

"How can you be so calm? All I feel is rage and hatred. I know you sense this. I know you can feel it too."

"I am as far from calm as I can possibly manage. But I have spent the last sixteen years drowning in that rage you are feeling right now. None of this will end if you kill him, but if I defeat him, then I *can* end what he has done to these people.

Right now, that is all I can do to manage what I am feeling. Aramecia, release him."

Aramecia turned her gaze on Magnus and he could see the tears that formed in her eyes. He could finally sense what she'd hid from him before. Her pain was just as heavy, if not more so than his own. He thought back to his first encounter with her outside of Grithala. He couldn't make sense of it then, but he now understood the sorrow he felt from her back then.

She released her grip on Cade's cloak and dropped him to the floor. He scrambled backward and to his feet. Magnus could feel his rage and his fear as he glared at Aramecia.

"You've already lost, Cade. No matter how this ends, you no longer hold the threat of power you once did."

"It's not over yet. Even if I die. I'll take you to Hell with me!" Cade charged Magnus in a blind rage.

Magnus dodged to the side and jammed his elbow in Cade's back. Cade turned and swung his fist at Magnus with no regard to how precise his attacks were. Magnus moved gracefully around his strikes before delivering a blow to the side of Cade's head. Cade stumbled and growled, jumping right back into the fight. Magnus side-stepped him again and hit him twice more, knocking him to the ground. He mounted him quickly and placed a few more punches where he could reach.

Cade groaned, bloodied, and beaten on the ground. Magnus held his fist up in the air above Cade's face. His chest heaved with every breath he took and the pain in his body had begun to take its toll once more.

"Surrender. No more lives need to be taken. Surrender and let this be done."

"I'd... rather...die," Cade muttered through pained breaths.

"There is no force in this world that would make me give you want. It's clear to everyone here who has won today. That is enough for me."

Magnus lifted himself up and turned to address the rest of the room. "Cade has been defeated. His hold on this town is broken. Elijah, tell the other council members that your seat has been reclaimed. I hand the Alchemy Guild back to you. Does anyone take issue with this?"

The room was silent. Magnus sighed and dropped his gaze. His body ached and he wasn't certain how much longer he could stand. He started to turn back to Aramecia when a guttural growl from behind him, followed by the sound of a sword on the stone floor, drew his attention. Cade lunged at him from the ground with a sword aimed straight at his chest.

A loud *crack* sounded through the room as a spear of fire pierced through Cade's chest. He came to a halt and looked down at the flaming protrusion. His eyes filled with terror and he cried out in pain, collapsing to the ground in smoldering flames. Aramecia stood behind him with her arm outstretched and her rage slowly fading, replaced by what Magnus could only call relief.

24

Forgiveness

The days following the battle with Cade were anything but quiet. The Alchemy Guild house became a mass of chaos as members scrambled to form search parties and hunt down any remaining members of the Emerald Blood who'd fled after Cade's death. Elijah went to work preparing for his reinstatement as a member of the High Council. There was some talk of the immediacy with which Magnus handed the seat back to Elijah, but little argument was brought forth with the satisfaction that Cade was, more or less, removed with proper procedure.

Despite the high spirits throughout the town following Cade's death, the atmosphere in the Alchemy Guild was a bit more sullen and heavy for Magnus and Neoma. Aramecia had become a difficult topic to discuss among those remaining in the guildhall. Credit for Cade's death went where it was due, but fear of someone who held her power was difficult to forget. Against Magnus's wishes, she was confined. The only compromise made was that her confinement was in their guest quarters and not the prison.

Magnus went to her every day. They sat together for hours, but despite her yearning for a family, for love, she found it difficult to connect with someone who was new to her and once presented as her enemy. Often times, there was immeasurable silence lingering between them. The daughter, taken from him long ago, and the father she thought killed soon after her birth.

"It truly is amazing how much you remind me of your mother. You could be her twin if one were to spare nothing but a glance." His voice was shaky, and his eyes darted between her and the floor.

"Cade told me much about her. About her time as an Ahndaele and the moniker she acquired. In truth, there was a time I wanted to be just like her. It's why I couldn't bring myself to kill needlessly for that man."

"I don't understand. Believe me, I am relieved that you have never taken a life, but even I have had to do so when I felt it necessary."

"You're wrong. As it is now. I have taken a life. At that moment, I felt calm. I felt at peace that he was gone, but now I can only imagine that others will fear me more knowing for certain that I could kill a man so easily." Aramecia pulled her knees into her chest and wrapped her arms around her legs. Magnus looked up at her and his heart sank for seeing the distance in her eyes.

"It is never easy on someone to take a life. Even if your own is being threatened or the life of one you love. What is easy on you is the lives that you have saved. My own, for instance. Had you not done what you did, he would have run me through, and I would have been powerless to stop him. We are together because you took action."

"Are we? We sit in this room together, but we sit as strangers. This is the first time I have even dared to hold a real conversation with someone that didn't involve death, war, or power. That is all I have ever known, yet for some reason, I never wanted any of it. I took what I could from Cade in the hopes that I would never have to set foot on another battlefield when this was all over. I even agreed to be his bride and walked a dark path that I can never come back from. I know you are my father, but I am not the daughter that you traveled all this way to save. For that I am sorry, but it cannot be helped."

Magnus chuckled as her voice faded. Aramecia looked up at him, shocked that he could find humor in her words. He shook his head and inched closer to her. He held his hand out and waited until she placed her palm against his.

"When you were taken from me, you were less than a year old. I could hold you with one hand and your eyes were taking in everything the world had to offer for the first time. You were unburdened and new to the experience of life. For the first five years that I searched, that was the daughter I might have hoped to find, but I am not so naive that I believed you would be the same unburdened little girl when I finally saw you again. I did not know who I would discover when I finally found you. This may well be the furthest thing I expected, but it is not someone I am ashamed of. Even in that den of hatred and destruction, you were a woman of your own strength and you sought your own path. I'm simply happy that I could sit here, like this, and hold your hand again."

"You searched for me? After all that time?" Aramecia asked.

"I would be lying if I said that I had not given up for some time. I never thought you were dead, but I had nowhere else that I could look on my own. I fell out of grace and if not for Neoma, I likely would not have had this chance."

"The woman who sought my life in the Grand Hall. You love her, don't you? It's subtle, but I often sense things that I can seldom interpret. Love and hatred are the only ones that I can identify."

A tear rolled down Magnus's cheek and he placed his free hand on top of hers. "You have my abilities. I suppose that would be the one you were naturally gifted."

"What is it?"

"You're an empath. You can sense other's emotions and read them. Though it takes time to untangle what each of those feelings is and what they mean. I can teach you."

"I can't imagine you would have the chance to do so," Aramecia whispered as she pulled her hand from Magnus's. She stood from the bed and walked over to the window, letting her fingers linger on the curtain as she peered through the glass. "Your love for Neoma is strong. You should be happy with her. After what I've done, I would only be a hindrance to that happiness. I burned her so that she would appear fatally wounded to the other members of the guild, but I did do her harm. I sat back and allowed countless others to die because I was too afraid to face the world on my own. Even if I were to restore her eye, it would not outweigh my sins."

"Perhaps not, but it is a start. I cannot absolve you of your wrongs that have been committed to others, but I can forgive you for what I have the power to forgive. For me, that is enough. Peace, that calm within yourself, will not come easy, but it will never have a chance to come if you do not have the courage to take the first step." Magnus stood up and walked towards the door. "I'll be back in a moment."

He shut the door behind him and in a few minutes, he returned with Neoma and Elias. They stepped into the room and the air filled with an almost tangible tension. Aramecia's eyes locked onto the floor at Neoma's feet. She stood with her hands cradled in front of her and Magnus couldn't help but see her as a scared little girl. All of the haughtiness she exhibited over their previous encounters seemed to dissipate without Cade's influence. He could no longer see the terrifying witch. Only a teenage girl who had never known kindness until now.

"When I was a little girl, I lived in a small village at the edge of Astoria's territory," Neoma spoke, stepping closer to Aramecia. "One day, a bandit guild walked into my home and they told my father, the village chief, that everything was theirs now. Our village had no warriors. We were a small tribe of seers and healers. The only weapon in our village was a knife, carved from the bone of a bear. My knife. One night, while all the bandits slept, I crept into their cabin and I could have easily killed every single one of them. Right then and there, their occupation would have ended. I had the power and the opportunity, but I didn't. I thought that, had I fought back, I would have nowhere else to go. The only people who want a killer among them, are killers themselves."

"So, I left. I went home and I slept in my bed, clutching the knife under the pillow and I cried." She grabbed Aramecia's hand and waited until she could look her in the eyes. "The next day the bandits saw my footprints and they gathered the village and asked them who it was that came upon them in their sleep. I was so frozen in fear that I could not bring myself to take responsibility for my actions. Because I couldn't, the bandits slaughtered everyone in my village and left the children so that we would never forget what they had done. When they left, the Royal Army showed up, but they were too late. I held my dead father and mother for hours, realizing that they had died because of me. They died because, twice, I stood by and could not do what needed to be done. I think about that almost every day."

"You never told me that story," Magnus said.

"I've never told anyone how I truly ended up in that orphanage. Not even Yeseni."

"I don't understand. Why are you telling me this?" Aramecia asked.

"Because that was my sin. That is the pain that I have to live with for the rest of my life and no one can forgive me for that. Just like you. I cannot forgive you for allowing my men to die, but I do understand why someone with all your strength could feel powerless. It is for that reason – that and your father's love – that I will not hate you. What you've done is wrong, but even with all your power, you're still a child. You have your whole life to do good despite the past."

Tears spilled from Aramecia's eyes. She fell into Neoma's arms and cried out in sorrow. Neoma wrapped her arms around her and let her spill out what she had held in for years.

Aramecia buried her head in Neoma's chest and whispered endless apologies through her muffled sobs.

After a few minutes, she pulled back and wiped her tears away. She looked up at Neoma's bandaged face and Magnus felt her deep regret wash over him. She reached up, placing her palm against the freshly wrapped bandages, and closed her eyes. For a moment, nothing happened. Then, a bright white light emanated from her palm, filling the room with a warm glow. After a few seconds, she pulled her hand away and opened her eyes.

Neoma felt the side of her face and quickly unwrapped the bandages. Beneath them, she could finally feel her skin. Her face had been restored, just as Aramecia had said. The wound to her eye and every inch of her injuries had vanished as though they never happened.

Neoma looked down and smiled at the pitiable, innocent look in Aramecia's eyes. "It's a start. Thank you."

"I don't mean to cut in on this touching family moment of the reformed witch and her bonding time with her new mother, but word from the High Council did come in earlier today," Elias spoke up. "They've agreed to let her go. So long as she never comes back into Reissgard's territory. You're free, girl."

"Truly? That's their only requirement?" Magnus asked.

"She put a flaming spear through Cade's chest. It put them in a pretty forgiving mood." Elias shrugged his shoulders and his lips spread in a sideways smile. "The real question is, where do you plan to go?"

"Wherever it is," Ember chimed in as she stepped out of

the hallway, "We'll take you. We've prepared a carriage. It's best we get going at once."

25

A Place to Call Home

The carriage ride out of Reissgard could only be described as hectic. Throngs of citizens bombarded them with thanks and attempted to repay them for their service. Cheers for the heroes of Reissgard filled the city with boisterous celebration. Even Aramecia, the witch who had once been feared by them all, was acknowledged for having betrayed the tyrant who kept the people under his thumb. Every man, woman, and child was in high spirits knowing that their kingdom could begin its journey to recovery.

Outside of the gates, members of various guilds mobilized in their pursuit of the remnants of the Emerald Blood. Magnus peered through the mass of people and spotted the Alchemy detachment, led by Freyr. She glanced over her shoulder and they both gave a solemn salute.

Once they were across the bridge, Ember pulled the carriage to a stop and turned to face the others. "All right? Where we headed?"

Magnus and Neoma exchanged a glance before turning to

Elias. Elias sighed and leaned into Ember, whispering into her ear. He leaned back as the carriage lurched forward once more and they were back on the road. Elias crossed his arms on his chest and shut his eyes.

"Where are we headed?" Magnus asked.

"Well, we can't very well go back to Astoria. What we've done here is far bigger than we first set out to accomplish. Word will spread quickly, and we will be seen as traitors for aiding a rival kingdom."

"I suppose so. We'll have to find a new home. Though I suppose that would not have been a bad idea in the first place. The place is filled with shadows. May well be best to begin anew."

"Yes, though I will have to return eventually. At least in secret. I would not forgive myself not to check in on her."

Magnus knew he spoke of Rhaste. The words made him smile. He thought of who Elias was before they left Astoria and felt he could barely recognize the man as he was now. The protective aura he exuded was more like that of a father than the cold-hearted assassin he tried to emulate over the years. He couldn't be certain which he was all along, but he was glad to know this one suited him well.

"You've still not answered the question of where we are going," Neoma chimed in.

"Right, well I suppose I thought it would be blatantly obvious. Where better to lay low than an insignificant little village where we already have an ally?" Elias responded.

"We're going back to Yeseni? Will she not be bothered by having us stay with her?" Magnus asked.

"To the same village, yes. I imagined you all would come

up with that destination on your own, so I had the foresight to send her a crow the day after the grand hall incident." He opened his eyes and glanced over at Magnus, Neoma, and Aramecia. "She's not particularly hoping for anymore extended guests, so she did us one better. I suppose you'll just have to wait and see."

He leaned back with a smile on his face. Everyone else was left in confusion, but after several attempts, it was clear he was unwilling to give them any more information. They spent the rest of the trip in idle conversation, talking more with Aramecia about life after they settled into their new home. She was, for the most part, calm and complacent, but Magnus could feel the anxious excitement she felt at escaping from her former life.

When they arrived in Yeseni's small hillside village, they had only a few seconds of quiet before Yeseni burst from her cabin and launched herself into Neoma's arms.

"Oh blessed! I'm so happy to see ya again! Oh my, yer eye is fixed! Yer all back alive! How wonderful! Oh, there's new people! Who are ya? And you? Oh, welcome back!"

Everyone except Aramecia laughed at her excited outburst. Eventually, everyone returned Yeseni's sentiments and welcomes. Once she had given her hugs to familiar faces, though rather reluctantly returned by Elias, she pranced over to Ember and Aramecia, studying their faces closely.

"So, y'all are fresh faces, hmm? Magnus here ain't gone and picked up any new lovers I hope," she said as she scanned them both. Her eyes settled on Aramecia and her face lit up. "No wait, this one's too young for that. Don't tell me... is this!"

She turned to Magnus with a smile spread wide across her

face. He chuckled and stepped forward to introduce her. "Yes, this is my daughter, Aramecia. It's been many years, but she has returned to me."

"By the ancestors, how wonderful!" Yeseni threw her arms around Aramecia and hopped around with her dangling in her grip.

"Pleasure. Please release me. I fear for both our safety if you do not," Aramecia choked out through rattled breaths.

"Apologies. I'm just so damned excited when people don't die. It's wonderful, ain't it? Now, come with me, everyone. Leave the cart here. You can move yer things later. Got a bit of a surprise for ya."

She turned and gestured for everyone to follow her. Yeseni skipped through the dirt walkways with her usual pep. She led them a few meters down the path before stopping in front of a wooden cabin that was slightly larger than her own. She spun around and held her arms out wide, smiling from ear to ear.

"Welcome home everyone!" she cheered.

"What?" Neoma asked.

"This! It's yours! Elias told me y'all were coming back so I had this place spruced up for ya. Don't get me wrong. Yer family of Neoma's so yer family o' mine as well, but I need my own space. So, here ya go!" She swung her arms forward and back again to gesture to the cabin once more, but everyone was still left in stunned silence.

"Um, Yeseni. When you told me you had secured our lodgings, I thought you meant a small home. We can't possibly pay the sum for a place like this," Elias spoke up.

Yeseni spat out laughing and gripped her sides. She wiped

a tear from her eye and addressed them again. "We ain't got no sort of money round here. We pay for everythin' by barter. You got land. We just ask you make yaselves useful. That's all there is to it. Head on in. I put some of my old furniture in there, but y'all can replace it as ya want. Just thought I'd make it a bit more homely for the newlyweds."

"Um, we're not married as of yet. Though I suppose if we've already secured a living space that would be the next logical step," Magnus explained.

"We don't have to rush. We've only just got here, and I know you and your daughter have a lot of catching up to do. We can get married at any time. I'm going nowhere."

"If it's all the same to you," Aramecia interjected, "I'd like to get to know you as well, Neoma. I've never had a mother. Not one that I knew. If it were alright with you, I'd like to come to think of you as my own."

Neoma's mouth hung open and tears formed in her eyes. She smiled and nodded her head.

"Aww, that's so freakin' cute," Yeseni exclaimed. Everyone turned their eyes to her, and her face turned bright red. "Sorry. Suppose I ruined a bit of a moment there. Anyhow, no putting off the wedding. Elias told me that too. I got yer arch being built by the botanist, so all ya have to do is choose who's doing the proclaimin', and who's helpin' with all the other fancy bits."

"Well, I suppose that makes things a bit easier. Elias, would you—"

"It will be a cold day in the Hell before I officiate a wedding," Elias blurted out coolly.

"Well, Ember?" Magnus asked.

"Fuck it. Got nothing better to do before I head back," Ember replied.

"Then who's going to set everything up?" Neoma asked.

Yeseni bounced up and down with her hand in the air. Neoma scanned the cabin, pretending like she couldn't see her best friend calling for her attention.

"I'm gonna damn well do it whether ya call on me or not!" Yeseni growled after Neoma's eyes passed over her twice.

"Alright, alright," Neoma chuckled then turned to Magnus. "I guess we're getting married."

"I have nothing to wear," Magnus replied.

26

Epilogue

In truth, that's where my story comes to an end. We did get married. That much I suppose is plainly obvious, but it was more than marriage for me. My life began anew the day that we exchanged our vows. I honestly can't even remember what we said. All I do remember is looking into her eyes and realizing that I felt something coming out of *me* that I hadn't felt in such a long time. Not happiness, or joy. It wasn't even love that surprised me. It was peace. It was serenity.

After we were wed, the village threw us a wonderful feast. Though with a small place with no more than twenty people, I suppose 'feast' is a relative word. Either way, it was wonderful. It was there that I made a promise to always protect my home and my family. It was true. When this all began, family was something I told myself that I didn't have. Now I had my wife, Neoma. I had my daughter, Aramecia, though there are still days when that is not easy. I had my brother, Elias. I had the excitable Yeseni, and even Ember felt like family to me, though I could never confirm that she felt the same.

More importantly, some weeks after our wedding, Yeseni was able to sense a new life among us. Our family would grow by one more. With news of Neoma's pregnancy, more announcements followed. I vowed to give up the battlefield; only to raise my fists if danger approached the people I love. I suppose you could say I couldn't risk it. Not again.

Ember had finally chosen to return to Reissgard. However, with her, Elias chose to leave too. He was searching to repair a family of his own. His father offered him a place at his side before we left, and I suppose he'd decided to accept. I didn't blame him. In fact, I encouraged him. So, when the sun rose the next day, they were gone.

So, you might be asking yourself, why did I make it point about pessimism so early in this story? The answer is simple. It's because I am not a pessimist. After hearing my story, can you blame me for looking at the world through such distrustful eyes? Can you blame me for still holding anger in my heart?

I love everything that I found on this journey, but outside of the walls of my home, outside of this small little unnamed village, the world continues to be rotten. I know it, but I have chosen to protect what I can protect. As it is now...

That's my family.

 Matrell Wood is a novelist and writer of various fantasy and science fiction works. Currently working on his Bachelor of Fine Arts in Creative Writing at Full Sail University, he has multiple well-received credits for his series *Haos Academy* as well as his novella *A Conversation with Grim*.

The stories that Matrell writes are all part of a collective universe chronicled in his platform, The Ahndrian Archives. Every story expands the universe and gathers a host of characters who are as interesting as they are flawed. As new stories are added, the web of connections is formed, and characters find themselves in different times and places.

Website: https://ahndrianarchives.com/
Facebook: https://www.facebook.com/TheAhndrianArchives/
Instagram: https://www.instagram.com/theahndrianarchives/
Twitter: https://twitter.com/ahndrianarchive

CPSIA information can be obtained
at www.ICGtesting.com
Printed in the USA
JSHW041120150121
10946JS00008B/201